the ISLAND of BEYOND

the ISLAND *of*
BEYOND

ELIZABETH ATKINSON

CAROLRHODA BOOKS
MINNEAPOLIS

Carolrhoda Books
A division of Lerner Publishing Group, Inc.
241 First Avenue North
Minneapolis, MN 55401 USA

For reading levels and more information, look up this title at www.lernerbooks.com.

The images in this book are used with the permission of: © Skip Brown/National Geographic/Getty Images (campfire); © iStockphoto.com/kentarcajuan (frame); © iStockphoto.com/moggara12 (starry sky); © iStockphoto.com/gepard001 (bird).

Main body text set in Bembo Std regular 12.5/17.
Typeface provided by Monotype Typography.

Library of Congress Cataloging-in-Publication Data

The Cataloging-in-Publication Data for *The Island of Beyond* is on file at the Library of Congress.
ISBN 978-1-4677-8116-9 (hardcover)
ISBN 978-1-4677-9557-9 (EB pdf)

Manufactured in the United States of America
1 – SB – 12/31/15

In memory of
my grandmother,
Louise, who carried
her easel from
Brittany to Maine,
and painted a
beautiful life.

Come away, O human child!
To the waters and the wild

—William Butler Yeats

CHAPTER ONE

"Don't you understand? He needs this, Amy."

"But for the whole month, Jonathan?"

"What else has he been doing with his summer so far? School's been out for a week, and he does nothing but sit around. A change like this will make all the difference."

I was lying in bed, reading the latest *Revengenators* comic book on my tablet, when I heard my parents start to argue about me again. It was strange how they assumed I couldn't hear them, as if closing my bedroom door at night meant I had suddenly gone deaf.

"Martin is fine," said my mom.

My father snorted, the same noise he made when

a politician was interviewed on the news or when an umpire made a bad call. "I'm not changing my mind, Amy. Everything's already settled."

What was already settled? What was he talking about? Dad was always making decisions without telling Mom or me ahead of time, but this sounded more serious than usual.

The kitchen grew quiet. I glanced at the clock on my nightstand and saw that it was ten o'clock. The time my parents move down into the basement family room so Dad can watch those crime shows filled with blood and guts, while Mom knits on the couch and drinks wine with lots of ice cubes.

The air conditioning kicked in as I turned off my lamp, feeling totally confused. What was Dad planning? I picked up my laser pen, which I kept hidden under a fuzzy green pillow. I sleep with three pillows—a regular one for my head, a little striped cushion to hug while I sleep, and then the fuzzy green pillow, which I use to hide Lego accessories and my miniature Rubick's Cube and interesting things I find but feel like I shouldn't show anyone. Especially not my father.

I shined the bright laser pen at my bookcase where I had assembled the village of Martinville over a year ago. The town was getting so big I was considering relocating it to the top of my bureau.

When I turned nine years old, Dad had given me his prized childhood collection of brownish-greenish soldiers, which he'd inherited from his father, my grampy. Dad assumed I would set up battle scenes and construct forts to blow up and conquer, like he had done with his little brother, Jason, when they were kids. The problem was my father had been a kid a really long time ago and no one did that stuff anymore. Besides, I didn't have a brother or a sister to boss around like Dad did. It was just my parents and me.

So for a long time I left the box to gather dust on a shelf in my closet. Until one day Mom told me that it hurt Dad's feelings that I never even tried to play with the old brownish-greenish soldiers. She suggested I come up with some creative game or project to include them, which would make Dad happy.

That's when I decided to redesign them with markers and make them ordinary people so I could play "town" instead of "war." Except that didn't seem to make my dad happy at all.

"What did Martin do to Grampy's soldiers?!" I heard him holler one night down in the kitchen after

I had gone to bed. There'd been silence after that, which meant Mom had probably poured Dad a glass of beer and pushed him toward the basement stairs to watch his crime shows.

"Good night, Baby Tim, Mayor Niceman, and Miss Puffy," I whispered in the direction of the bookcase.

Every evening I chose three different townspeople to wish good night.

"I'm sure we'll all get to the bottom of whatever's going on. So there's no need to worry. Happy dreams, everyone."

The day was officially over after I lowered the laser pen beam from the ceiling, past the town, down to the floor . . . as if I had made the real sun set over Martinville.

Everyone was safe, at least until tomorrow.

CHAPTER TWO

The next morning I was surprised to find Dad eating scrambled eggs and toast in the kitchen. He usually left for work before I even woke up, especially in the summer when I slept later.

"Why are you still here?" I asked.

He closed his laptop and took a sip of coffee.

"You sound disappointed. Aren't you glad to see me?"

Truthfully, I wasn't glad at all to see him first thing in the morning. I was used to having just Mom around. She knew exactly how I liked a banana sliced on my cereal. Now that school was out, she took the summer off from her part-time job at the fabric store so she could be home with me, even though I was eleven and didn't need supervision. I mostly sat on the couch in the basement playing video games or reading new *Revengenators* comics.

"Did you get fired?" I asked, avoiding my father's question.

"Martin," said Mom as she scraped dried egg from the frying pan into the sink, "don't be disrespectful."

"I wasn't being disrespectful."

"For your information," said Dad, "I took the day off to be with you."

A ball of knots formed in my stomach. Spending the day with my father never ended well.

That's when I noticed the stack of folded maps sitting on the kitchen table next to Dad's plate. And the two pieces of luggage leaning against the back door: one big suitcase with wheels and a small duffel bag with a sports team logo. Why would we need luggage for a one-day outing?

"Wait. Are we going somewhere?"

"Let's just say I've got a *terrific* opportunity for you, buddy," Dad replied through a mouthful of eggs.

I dug my hand into my left pajama pocket to check on Mr. Little, a very tiny stuffed mouse I got in my Easter basket when I was five. He watched over Martinville at night and secretly kept me company during the day. "It's not soccer camp again, is it? Because there's no way I'd survive that a second time . . . "

"Nope, this is something completely different." With his right sneaker my father shoved the chair closest to me. "Sit down, Martin. Let's have a man-to-man."

I didn't like where this was going, but I sat. My mother instantly slipped a bowl of cereal in front of me, topped perfectly with bananas.

"Are we taking a vacation?" I asked.

Mom clapped her hands together. "That's a wonderful way to think of it!"

"To think of what?"

"*Amy,*" Dad snapped, "stop sugarcoating everything all the time."

"What are you sugarcoating?" I asked.

"Eat your cereal, honey, and let your father explain," said Mom, who was now rewashing the dishes she'd already washed.

"I'm not hungry. Just tell me what's going on!"

My dad cleared his throat and shook his head as if he were about to make a painful confession. "Well— here's the thing, Martin. It's time for you to learn how to be—um, to learn how to be more of a . . . "

"More of a *what*?"

He lowered his voice.

"You need to figure out how to be more of a boy. A normal boy. Do you understand what I'm saying?"

"Not really."

Mom rushed over from the sink, drying her hands on a dish towel. "What your father is trying to say, honey, is that he would like to see you spending more time outdoors this summer."

"Huh?" Now I was completely confused.

"Amy, please stop interfering!"

This is exactly why I preferred my father to be at work. The world felt upside down whenever he was around. Mom knew how to make everything feel better. Calmer.

"Fine," she said, then threw down the dish towel and left the room.

At that point I felt like I couldn't breathe. It wasn't that I was afraid of Dad or that I thought he didn't love me. But nothing I did or said or felt ever seemed right when I was with him.

"See these?" He picked up an old folded map from the pile on the table.

I nodded cautiously.

"I have seven maps, one for each state you and I will be driving through."

"We're *driving* across seven states?"

"That's right!"

I said nothing for several seconds. Then: "Why would we do that?"

"To get where we're going!"

Now I couldn't breathe *plus* the room began to spin. Soccer camp had been bad enough, but at least it had been close to home.

I gathered all my courage and squeezed Mr. Little. "So where are we going?"

"You remember Aunt Lenore?"

"I guess. The old lady who lives in Maine?"

I'd never actually met Aunt Lenore, but Dad talked about her whenever he reminisced about his perfect childhood. She lived on some kind of private island in the middle of a lake in Maine, where Dad and my uncle Jason had spent every perfect summer of their perfect childhood. Technically, she wasn't even Dad's aunt. She was Grampy's second cousin or something . . .

"*The old lady who lives in Maine?* More like the classiest, most elegant woman I've ever known. Impeccably dressed every single day, and tea at four, even up there in the Maine wilderness. They don't make 'em like Aunt Lenore anymore."

I knew he meant this as a compliment, but I was fine with the way people were now.

"Did she die?" I asked, figuring she must be at least a hundred years old.

"What? Of course not. I mean, she will someday, but for now she's alive and well. In fact, I just spoke with her on the phone yesterday, which brings me back to this terrific opportunity!"

I glanced at the stack of maps, at the luggage, at my father grinning way too hard. I had a bad feeling I knew where this was headed.

"It turns out that you, *you lucky kid*, have been invited to spend the entire month of July with her on Lake Nevermore! No boring Delaware for you this summer. What do you say to that?"

I had nothing to say to that.

Instead I ran to the closest bathroom and locked the door.

CHAPTER THREE

"MARTIN?"

Mom knocked for the third time.

"We'd like to talk this over, sweetheart. Come out, please, and eat your cereal."

But I wasn't going anywhere. I would cry on the shower floor for the rest of the summer if that's what it took to stay in Delaware.

"You see what I'm saying, Amy?" I heard my father say. "He's bawling like a you-know-what."

"Can't you see this is *your* fault, Jonathan? You have no idea how to talk to him."

"I CAN HEAR YOU!"

"Listen, buddy, be reasonable," said Dad, trying a new approach. "Those summers your uncle Jason and I spent at Aunt Lenore's house on Beyond Island were the best times of my life."

I'd heard that before. The way Dad talked about those trips, you'd think he'd been given free reign at Comic-Con every year. But Beyond Island? Lake Nevermore? They sounded like settings for a horror movie, not a summer vacation.

"I promise you, you're gonna love it!"

"No I won't—I'll hate it hate it HATE IT!" I managed to shriek between deep sobs.

On the other side of the door, Mom lowered her voice. "Couldn't we give him one more day, Jonathan, to take it all in?"

"And exactly *how* would I explain that to Aunt Lenore?"

Just then the door popped open and the shower curtain whipped back. My father frowned at me, his hands planted on his hips. Behind him, Mom stood holding a tiny key.

"You and I hit the road in forty minutes," Dad said flatly. "We need to make it to the freeway before the lunch rush in Wilmington."

I curled my whole self into the smallest ball possible as panic washed over my entire body. Dad stepped into the shower and knelt down in front of me.

"Listen to me, Martin. This is the chance of a lifetime. You'll get to spend an entire month doing all kinds of amazing things—learning to climb the highest tree and catching enormous frogs and holding your breath for two whole minutes while you explore the bottom of the lake!"

Hugging my legs as tight as I could, I yelled into my chest, "You *know* I hate all those things! I would never do any of that."

"Exactly," said my father. "Do the opposite of what you would normally do. Just trust me on this, Martin."

"*NOOO*," I wailed. "I'm NOT going!"

He groaned loudly.

"Will you please leave and let me handle this, Jonathan?" said Mom as she reached in and pulled him out of the shower. "You're making everything worse."

Dad almost tripped as he stepped back. "Well, hurry up," he hissed, "we have a very tight schedule!"

He slammed the door as he left.

I kept my head buried in my arms, refusing to budge. Mom bent down and gently rested her hand on my foot. For a second, I thought I had won the battle.

"Your father's right. You have to trust us, honey. We wouldn't send you somewhere dangerous or unpleasant."

What? I couldn't believe she was in on this too. No matter how much my parents argued about me, I always knew Mom was on my side.

"And sweetheart, this is very important to your father. It would be awfully rude of us to accept Aunt Lenore's generous offer and then go back on our word. You wouldn't want her to get angry with your dad, would you?"

"Why does Dad care what she thinks more than he cares what *I* think?"

"Aunt Lenore and the island mean a lot to him, Martin. And Lenore doesn't have any—any direct descendants, so your dad is the closest family she has. He wants to make sure he stays on good terms with her."

"Then why doesn't *he* go visit her?"

"You know he can't take more than a day or two off of work at a time. And besides, he thinks this will be good for you."

Good for me? Soccer camp was supposed to be good for me. Swimming lessons were supposed to be good for me. All the things I was bad at, all the things I didn't want to do, somehow were supposed to be good for me just because Dad said so.

"I tell you what," she whispered. "Give it a chance for a week. And then, if you still want to come home, I'll drive up there and pick you up."

I stopped crying. A week was a long time, but it was a whole lot better than a month.

I straightened my back and wiped my nose with my sleeve. "Five days?" I countered.

"Six."

"Starting now?"

She nodded.

"Deal," I sighed, and I let her kiss the top of my head.

I spent my last moments at home gathering important supplies I couldn't live without, although Mom said I could bring only one pillow and not all three. I made my bed and lined up my shoes in the closet. Last and most important, I gave everyone in Martinville a pep talk.

"Now it's only for six days, so no need to panic," I explained as I sniffed back tears. "Mayor Nice-man will be in charge while I'm gone. And since

Mr. Little will be traveling with me, Sir Blink will stand guard."

No one said anything—I could tell they were as in shock as I was. In the end I decided the humane thing to do was to cover the entire town with a light blanket since I wouldn't be able to mark the sun rising and setting each day. I figured this was similar to a temporary state of hibernation. I wished I could do the same thing to myself.

By ten thirty, my father and I were driving north on I-95.

"I can't believe we've never done this before!" said Dad. "Two cool guys hitting the road together, heading to the North Country, taking in the view, free as birds."

I, for one, *could* believe we had never done this before, because it was the last thing on earth I would ever choose to do. I stared out the window and absorbed each freshly mowed lawn and orderly flower bed we passed, as if I'd never see civilization again. Dad turned on the radio and found one of his favorite talk shows, the kind where raspy men yell at each other about sports.

I leaned forward and activated the GPS. "What's the name of the town?" I asked.

"Aidenn," he murmured in a dreamy voice. "Aidenn, Maine." Then he snapped out of it and added, "But no GPS on this trip! We're using real maps, the way life used to be when I was a kid."

I could never understand grown-ups' obsession with *the way life used to be*, as if slower and more boring were somehow better qualities.

"Can you just spell it?" I asked. "I want to check something."

"A-i-d-e-n-n," he said, "but check it quickly and then turn it off. I want you to have the full experience of traveling back in time."

According to the GPS, the drive was 628.23 miles and was estimated to take eleven hours and fifty-four minutes. Add in the restroom and fast food stops, and we would arrive in the dark, spooky woods of Maine well after midnight. My heart started to pound. Even in the suburbs, where the streets and homes were always well-lit, nighttime gave me the creeps.

"I think I need to go to the bathroom," I moaned.

"You can make it until noon."

"But Mom says I have an unusually weak bladder."

Dad rolled his eyes. "We'll pull off the road soon and eat our sandwiches."

"Can't we eat indoors at a restaurant where we can wash our hands?"

The veins around my father's knuckles swelled as he squeezed the steering wheel. It didn't seem like he was having as much fun as he claimed. "We'll have dinner at a restaurant tonight at the hotel I booked in Connecticut."

"A hotel?"

"I want to arrive at Aunt Lenore's house in the daylight tomorrow, so you get the full lay of the land!"

The thought of a clean, tidy hotel room and free Wi-Fi—not to mention avoiding the scary outdoors at night—was enough to settle my bladder. I plugged earbuds into my phone and played a game of Mutant Minnows as my dad joined the shouting match happening on the radio. Thankfully, I couldn't hear a word.

CHAPTER FOUR

The hotel was actually a rundown motel and the lobby smelled like wet cats, but I managed to sleep pretty well. We "hit the road" by eight the next morning, and even though the management couldn't find any of my favorite cereal brands in their kitchen, they did have ripe bananas and two percent milk. So the day was off to a reasonably normal start.

By the time we passed through Massachusetts and New Hampshire and crossed the Maine border I had accumulated ten trillion points on Mutant Minnows, the most you can win. I figured I should save my other games for the long boring hours I would have to spend at Aunt Lenore's house over the next five days.

"Maine is enormous," said Dad. "Just look at the map!"

We went through this every time we crossed state lines, the grand opening of the next map. And each time I pretended to look.

"Uh-huh," I automatically replied.

"We still have another 162 miles to go, which isn't even halfway up the state!" he exclaimed. "I bet you could fit fifty Delawares into one Maine!"

He said this as if size alone made Maine superior to Delaware. But so far I had seen nothing other than pine trees and gas stations.

My father rolled down his window. "AH!" he said after drawing in a deep breath. "Smell that! Maine air! The best in the world!"

The blast of wind sent the maps flying.

"Can you please close that before we lose everything we own?"

Dad frowned as he pressed the button. After a couple of minutes he glanced over at me and patted my leg, something he hadn't done in a really long time.

"When I was your age, Jason and I spent countless afternoons on the island, building forts out of branches and any leftover planks we could find in the shed. And at the designated time we would attack each other with slingshots and pine-cone bombs."

I knew where this was going. More stories about his amazing childhood—boring stories that I'd heard a thousand times before. I peered down at my phone and searched for new games.

"Those were the days! I know it's different now, Martin. I know most kids don't spend hours out-doors, unsupervised, left to their own devices . . ."

Suddenly, I could barely get a signal on my phone, so I held it up toward the windshield.

"But I think something is lost when you don't get that chance to challenge yourself against nature, to see how far you can go using nothing but your mind, body, and spirit."

He was starting to sound like a spokesman for the Boy Scouts, another of our failed attempts to bond as father and son.

"What's the big deal about nature?" I finally responded. "So what if kids don't do all that outdoors stuff anymore?"

Dad made a long sighing noise like a slowly deflat-ing balloon. Then he chewed on his bottom lip and tapped his right temple. "Because your mind goes soft," he whispered. "Everything turns to mush."

I didn't know what he was talking about since I was one of the smartest kids in my grade.

"Wait till you see the island, then you'll know what I mean. And the house! The oldest, biggest house in Aidenn. Classic nineteenth-century Victorian. Absolutely magnificent. I'm telling you, Martin, you're going to have the time of your life up there. The time. Of. Your. Life."

I reached for Mr. Little and exhaled.

During the next two hours, every new road we turned onto grew smaller and bumpier until we came to a tiny town with three buildings. An old wooden sign with the words *Welcome to Aidenn* hung from a tree next to a store called Only Market. My stomach clenched. We were here.

Dad turned right onto the very last street, nothing more than a dirt alley with lots of holes and rocks. Suddenly he stopped the car and blasted the horn twice.

"What was that for?" I asked.

"Only one vehicle at a time can fit down the lane," he replied, "so you have to honk twice before you start out at each end. If you hear someone honk back once, it means you need to stop and stay put as they're driving toward you. Isn't that a terrific system?!"

That word again.

"Yep, *terrific*."

No one honked back, so we ventured on, passing dirty creeks and the infinite woods. How many pine trees could there be in one state?

Eventually the road came to an *end*, and when I say end, I mean we literally came to the edge of a lake, so we were forced to stop. Dad pulled the car off to the side and parked under a large sagging tree branch.

"Hasn't changed a bit around here," he murmured. Then he jumped out, popped open the trunk, and grabbed our luggage.

"Wait!" I said. "Where's the house?"

My father grinned as he pointed at the water. I leaned across the driver's seat and squinted at a clump of trees far off in the liquid distance. Beyond that were mountains, all different sizes, standing at attention in one endless line.

"This is Lake Nevermore," he said and slammed the trunk. "And Beyond Island is out there in the middle of it."

"But where's the bridge?"

"That's the best part." He beamed. "We get to row over!"

"Row? Like in a rowboat?"

"You got it!" He walked toward a rickety red boat partly hidden behind a huge rock. "That's why they leave this here."

I hadn't signed up for that. Technically I hadn't signed up for any of this, but especially not the part about being in a boat and crossing deep water. How deep *was* it? Did Dad even know?

"Did we pack a life preserver?"

He knew perfectly well that I couldn't swim.

"Nah, you'll be fine. Believe me, you'd learn quicker than a tadpole if you accidentally fell in."

I was instantly seasick—or maybe just homesick.

I pulled Mr. Little out of my pocket and stared into his sad, teeny-tiny eyes.

"Five days," I whispered, "just five more days until Mom picks us up."

CHAPTER FIVE

Dad shoved the old red boat into the water and told me to take the front seat. I held my breath as I climbed over the words printed along the side: *To Beyond and Back*. Dad faced backward and rowed with two huge wooden paddle things, whistling like a sailor, while I gripped the bench and squeezed my eyes shut.

Our family said prayers only during the typical times when you were supposed to, like before Thanksgiving dinner and at the beginning of baseball season, which involved a special prayer Dad made us say for the Baltimore Orioles. But about a million prayers popped into my head all at once as we crossed deep, dark, wavy Lake Nevermore. Prayers like *Please God, don't let me get sucked over the edge of this boat into a vortex and drown* and *Please God, don't let a mutant minnow plunge into this boat and eat my eyeballs.*

Dad's rowing and whistling eventually stopped, and so did the swoosh of the water, so I opened one eye. Finally we had reached an old dock. The sides were covered in green slime, and a big black bird stood at the far end. It squawked, then flew away just before Dad pulled in the rower thingies and grabbed the closest pole.

"I could use a little assistance here, Martin. Grab the tie-offs in the bow."

"Huh?"

He frowned, then mumbled, "Just hand me that rope behind you."

By the time we climbed out of the old red boat with our luggage, I realized I was exhausted from so much stress and activity. Now I prayed that Aunt Lenore had a comfortable couch in front of the TV so I could relax the rest of the afternoon.

It was pointless to try rolling my suitcase on the ground, since the dirt trail up to the house was narrow and rocky and choking with low scratchy plants. But the suitcase was too heavy for me to carry along with my backpack, so Dad switched with me since he had just the light overnight duffel bag.

"By the end of the month you'll have muscles big enough to carry all this stuff!"

I doubted that because (a) I was leaving in five days, and (b) muscles required exercise, which I planned to do very little of during my summer vacation.

Suddenly Dad bent toward the ground. "Look! I think those are blueberries!"

"Where?"

He pointed at a scrappy bush. "Maine's finest contribution to the produce aisle."

I wasn't impressed. "I like my berries in a little green box covered in plastic wrap."

Dad stood up and shook his head. "You see? That's exactly what's wrong with your generation. You have no connection to the outdoors. Everything comes to you prepackaged."

When the trail ended, we arrived at a large wood-shingled house with more wooden steps and a wide wooden porch. I was beginning to wonder if everything was made of wood in this state—if we would sleep on boards and eat twigs.

"There's the sign!" said Dad, pointing up at a long, thin, moss-covered slab of wood hanging over the porch. "*Welcome to the Great and Beautiful Be*—"

His voice dropped off as he squinted to get a better look. The far end of the sign had broken off.

"I think the *yond* is missing," I said.

Dad straightened and took a moment to study the rest of the gray house, which clearly wasn't as magnificent as he'd remembered. Dirty white shutters were hanging off cracked windows. Shingles had fallen from the steep roof, leaving bare patches covered in what seemed to be tiny plants. Dad forced himself to smile as we climbed the long set of wooden stairs to the front door.

"Look!" he exclaimed, seeing a bell the size of a melon suspended from the dark porch ceiling. "I can't believe she still has this!"

As soon as he rang it, a wrinkly old lady appeared behind the screen door. A mound of bluish-white hair sat on top of her head, and she wore a long faded pink dress covered in lace even though it was kind of hot and the middle of the afternoon.

"Who's making that racket?" she croaked.

"Aunt Lenore?"

The old woman's big buggy eyes got bigger and buggier. "What do you want?"

"It's, um, wonderful to see you," he said, unconvincingly. "I can't believe it's been so—"

"I have no idea who you are," she said, cutting him off, "so you can leave the same way you came."

What was going on? Did she just tell us to leave? My heart began to beat with excitement.

"Aunt Lenore, it's me, Jonny," said Dad as he pushed open the screen door.

She slammed it back so quickly she almost caught Dad's hand. "Excuse me, but I do not allow strangers to waltz into my home. And I am *not* interested in buying whatever it is you're selling!"

"I think you're a little confused, Aunt Lenore," said Dad in what was probably supposed to be a soothing voice. "We talked on the phone a couple of days ago. About my son, Martin? You suggested he spend the month of July here with you on Beyond, like Jason and I used to do."

"Why on earth would I want to spend my favorite month of the year with someone I've never met?" she inquired. "Now go away before I dial up the National Guard over in Waterville. I have connections with them, you know!"

Just as I was convinced a miracle was actually taking place—that my prayers had been answered and we could turn around and go home—someone else appeared behind the screen door. She was younger than Aunt Lenore but older than my parents, who were pretty old for parents.

"Is that you, Mr. Hart?"

"Tess, thank goodness. I think I've upset poor Aunt Lenore."

The old lady poked the screen with her long bony finger. "Now listen up, Mr. Whoever-you-think-you-are. I most certainly am not *poor*, and more important, I couldn't possibly be the aunt of some big, bulky, bald stranger like yourself."

I couldn't help giggling, but Dad frowned.

"Of course not, Lenore," said the lady named Tess. "Now come along with me and we'll get you settled."

She wrapped her arm around the old woman's shoulders and led her away from the door.

"Wait here, Mr. Hart," she whispered over her shoulder. "I'll be right back."

CHAPTER SIX

A few minutes later, Dad, Tess, and I sat together in a dark, musty living room. Even though the sun shone brightly outside, long heavy curtains blocked the daylight.

My father sat with his legs pressed tightly together, his hands on his knees as if he were a boy again. He smiled faintly as he scanned the room, probably searching for familiar objects from his childhood.

"As I explained on the phone, Lenore has been getting more and more forgetful lately," Tess explained in a hushed voice.

"Wait, you knew she was like this?" I said to Dad. In all his glowing descriptions of her, he definitely hadn't mentioned that she was losing her marbles.

Dad shot me an annoyed look. "I didn't know it was quite this bad."

"And it seems to be getting worse each day," said Tess. "I finally convinced her to agree to see a doctor later this month. I'm guessing it's dementia. Not really surprising at her age. Please don't take it personally."

"Poor Aunt Lenore," said Dad, shaking his head. "It's a shame she didn't even recognize me. We used to be very close."

"So is Aunt Lenore your sister?" I asked Tess.

"Oh my, no," she said.

Dad scowled at me as if I was supposed to know who everyone was.

"I've been working for Lenore and Ned for about twenty years now," Tess explained. "I guess you could say I'm the house manager."

"Uncle Ned?" my father groaned. "Don't tell me he still hangs around here. I thought he'd left the island years ago."

Just then a shadow moved across the window in the crack of light between the drapes. I walked over and peered through the clouded glass, but I saw nothing other than more trees.

"He's only here occasionally," said Tess, "mostly to take care of odd jobs around the property."

I turned around and asked, "Is Uncle Ned married to Aunt Lenore?"

"Good grief, no," Dad barked, as if explaining anything to me took too much effort. "Aunt Lenore's never been married. Ned's her younger brother, but they're nothing alike."

"We hardly ever see him, Mr. Hart," said Tess. "He stays in the cabin out back when he's here and he's very quiet."

I glanced over at Dad. "Is there something wrong with him?"

He grimaced. "Don't worry about it, Martin."

Tess stood up and changed the subject. "Would you like to see your bedroom, young man?"

"You mean I'm staying?" Was Dad really going to leave me here after everything Tess just told us? "Shouldn't you check again with Aunt Lenore first? I don't think she wants me around."

"Oh, she'll warm up to the idea in a few days," said Tess.

"That's right," said Dad, and then he lowered his voice. "When I was your age she could be pretty darn grumpy at times, but under that tough exterior she has a heart of gold. You just hang in there and do your best to get on her good side."

What was he talking about? How did getting on a crazy old lady's good side have anything to do with the amazing summer Dad seemed convinced I was going to have?

When I say the whole house was smelly and dark, I mean it was *really* smelly and dark, like the crawl space next to our basement. And cluttered too. I had never seen so many knickknacks and stacks of old books and antique furniture filling so many rooms. Dad kept pointing at stuff, thrilled to see that almost everything was where it had been when he was a kid. It was pretty obvious none of it had been dusted since then either.

I didn't pay too much attention to the tour, since I knew I would be gone by the end of the week. And I was trying really hard not to think about how creepy this house was.

"We'll take a look at the bedrooms upstairs next," said Tess. "Any questions so far, Martin?"

"Where do keep your TV?"

She wrinkled her eyebrows. "Lenore doesn't own one."

"Seriously?" I swallowed hard.

My father patted me on the back. "That's what makes this place so special," he said.

"What's so special about not owning a TV?"

He laughed. "Don't be rude, Martin."

I wasn't trying to be rude, but I needed to know how I was expected to entertain myself. "So do you stream shows online?"

Tess sighed. "I don't even know what that means." She looked at my father. "I'm afraid we're very far behind. Ned spent years trying to talk Lenore into getting a computer, but he gave up ages ago. Oh, and you'll have to use the landline if you want to check in with Martin while he's here. The cell service on the island is terrible. Not that the landline hasn't also failed us from time to time . . ."

I immediately checked my cell phone. *No signal.* My heart began to race. It was as if I were at the end of the earth, or back in the 1970s when Dad and his brother stayed here.

"Now you'll have more time to explore the great outdoors," said my father, who was grinning too hard again, "and maybe meet some of the other kids around here!"

He couldn't be serious. Was he really going to

leave me here with nothing to do?

"I'm afraid he won't find many appropriate playmates either," said Tess quietly. "With the way the economy has been, very few families have stayed."

That didn't matter to me, since I had no intention of making friends in the next few days. Besides, I hardly had any friends back in Delaware. But the thought of surviving almost a week with absolutely nothing to do was horrifying.

After climbing the narrow stairs to the second level, we passed creepy empty bedrooms as we walked down the slanted hallway toward the room where I would wait for the next 120 hours for Mom to arrive. I had to admit, this room felt a little better than the rest of the house, probably because the curtains were tied back. Sunshine and a light breeze flowed through the open windows. The enormous bed, with tall wooden posts at each corner, had been pushed up against the middle of the wall. The top of the mattress came up to my stomach.

"We haven't had guests in years," Tess said, as we stood in the center of the room. "I've tried to tidy it up, but you may discover a few dust bunnies."

"Terrific!" said Dad, his new favorite word. "I'll run down and get your suitcase from the porch. Be right back."

Suddenly, I was left alone with Tess. I didn't know what to say. She didn't either. I reached in my pocket and squeezed Mr. Little. For the first time in my life, I wanted my father more than anything, which was a strange feeling. Everything felt strange.

I peered out the window and saw a shadowy figure sneaking through the trees below. It was a small person wearing dark clothes and a black hood.

"Who's that?" I whipped around to ask Tess, but now she was gone too.

I rushed out to the hall just as Dad returned with my suitcase.

"You can't really leave me here!" I cried and clung to his waist.

He patted my back. "Come on, cheer up. You'll be fine. Tess will take good care of you. And I guarantee you're going to make lifelong memories."

"Not the kind of memories I'm going to want to remember!"

"Always the smart aleck," he laughed and peeled my arms from his body. "You know, you and Aunt

Lenore have that sarcasm in common. In fact I bet you two have a lot in common."

Being told I was a lot like a senile, grumpy old woman made me feel even worse. Right then the wind blew hard outside, rattling the floorboards and doorways.

"I'm serious, Dad. This is a humongous mistake. There is no way I can stay in this creepy house. I think I just saw a burglar, or maybe a ghost, out the window sneaking through the woods."

"You and your wild imagination," he said, knocking on my head. "This is what happens to your mind when you spend so much time playing video games."

But somewhere in his voice I could hear doubt, and he refused to look me in the eye. I knew he was also trying to convince himself that everything would be fine.

"You know, Martin," he continued, "I realize this place isn't what it used to be. It's quieter and everything has gotten a little rundown since Jason and I stayed here."

"*A little?* And that's another thing—you had your brother!"

I was on the verge of exploding into tears. This

was worse than anything else my father had forced me to do over the years, even worse than soccer camp.

"Now listen to me, son, you need to get a hold of yourself," he whispered directly into my face. "I'm counting on you to put your best foot forward. Aunt Lenore specifically asked me to bring you out here for a visit, even though she seems to have forgotten that at the moment. But I'm certain she wants to get to know you. And I wouldn't want to disappoint her."

I sniffed back more tears. "*Why?* Why does it matter so much? *You* haven't visited her in forever! Why should I have to?"

He took a deep breath and spoke very slowly. "Look, Martin, I would've loved to have spent more time here over the years. But Aunt Lenore hasn't really been accepting visitors for a while. I'll tell you what, though: I think having you with her this summer is going to change her mind. In fact, I think she may even be planning to leave us this island in her will. And the more you can do to . . . *encourage* her to entrust me with this property . . . the better."

I was stunned. And speechless. This was why he'd brought me here? To get on Aunt Lenore's "good side" so that he could get the island after she died? Was any of this about me at all?

"I know I can count on you, buddy," he added cheerfully, "so pull yourself together and do this for your old man! And I promise, I'll give you a call in a couple of days. You'll be just fine."

CHAPTER SEVEN

A few minutes later, I watched from the second-story window as Dad hurried down the trail toward the lake, which was barely visible through the trees. A wave of sadness, like I had never felt before, washed over my whole body.

I pulled Mr. Little out of my pocket. "What do we do now?"

"Would you like to take a walk around the property?" Tess's reply startled me. She was standing in the doorway holding a basket. "I can show you the best path down to the beach and we can get some vegetables from the garden for tonight's dinner."

"No thanks," I mumbled, determined to stay in this room for as long as possible.

I picked up my backpack and searched for my charger so I could plug it in and charge my phone. At least I had downloaded a couple games to play, the only thing that would keep me sane for the next 119 hours.

"How about a glass of milk?" Tess asked, reminding me I would have to eat and drink while I waited for Mom to come pick me up.

"Do you have ginger ale?"

"Just milk," she replied.

"Then I guess I'll have chocolate milk."

"No chocolate, I'm afraid."

What was wrong with these people? Hadn't they heard it was the twenty-first century? "Forget it," I moaned and continued rummaging through my stuff.

Tess pulled open the top drawer of the bureau. "Would you like help unpacking? There's plenty of space in the dresser."

"I'm not unpacking," I mumbled. "I'm just looking for something."

"Suit yourself. Call down if you need anything," she said and disappeared again.

Just as I started to panic that my charger was missing, I felt it at the bottom of the middle pocket.

I searched the walls for an outlet but didn't see one. After locating the one lamp in the room, I followed the cord behind the bed. I had to slide along the floor underneath the sagging springs to plug the charger into the wall. Tess was right about the gross dust bunnies. After sliding out, I changed my T-shirt and placed the dirty one in my hamper bag. Already down one shirt. Luckily I still had enough clean ones to last until the weekend.

Finally, I connected my phone to the charger, but as soon as I did, it made a terrifying noise.

PFZTT!

The end of the cord lit up and shot sparks. I disconnected the phone and pressed the power button—but nothing. I removed and replaced the battery—and still nothing! The tiny jack was burned black, my last link to civilization gone. My phone was fried.

I hurled myself across the giant bed, face-first into the moldy quilt, and sobbed. I didn't care who heard me. I didn't care what they said to me or thought of me or even did to me. I had never felt so sorry for myself in my entire life.

But as it turned out no one heard me, or if they did it didn't matter, because within seconds I had cried myself to sleep.

I woke hours later covered by the quilt, still wearing my clothes but not my sneakers. I scanned the dark room, and all at once I remembered where I was. My heart sank. I dug into my pocket for Mr. Little and held him to my face.

"Are you okay?" I whispered.

Except for the constant creaky noises, the old house was silent. I wished I could hear a honking car or a barking dog or at least one other kid's voice. Just then a shadowy figure moved past the bureau. I shrieked and whipped my head under the quilt and prayed I wouldn't be attacked. Several seconds later a light switched on.

"What in the world are you screaming about?" said Tess. She set a tray of food on the bureau and straightened my blanket.

"You scared me!" I replied.

"Apparently. We could hear you all the way downstairs."

"Downstairs? But weren't you just sneaking around here in the dark?"

"For your information, I never sneak around anywhere," she replied as she plumped my pillows.

"What you see is what you get. Now it's time to sit up and eat."

Her puckered lips and raised eyebrows made her look like a teacher.

"Tess?" I whispered. "Is this place haunted?"

"Goodness," she said as she slipped the tray of food onto my lap. "I think hunger is making you hallucinate. You missed dinner, but here's a bowl of soup for you, local quail with wild rice. Soothes the soul *and* the ghosts."

"Ghosts?"

She crossed the room and closed the windows. "I'm teasing you. I'm sure it was only the wind," she said and smiled. "Now come downstairs as soon as you're feeling better."

But I was determined not to leave that room except to use the crooked bathroom in the slanted hall. And I decided I would leave a small lamp on at all times to fend off any spooky night-lurking creatures. I tried to convince myself I had the flu, as if I were sick and cooped up in my bedroom back in Delaware. But it was nothing like that, since I'd have fun stuff to do there like watch shows on my laptop, read comics, and play games on my phone, not to mention all of Martinville to keep me company.

The first thing Mr. Little and I did after I finished the strange soup was investigate every dusty corner of the room.

Next to the bed was a small side table with a single drawer, which contained one shiny flat rock. When I picked it up, the rock dissolved, leaving a pile of sparkling crumbs.

We opened more drawers in the tall bureau, but they were smelly and empty. I skimmed the stack of old books piled on a shelf in the corner, but the titles were boring.

And then I noticed part of a newspaper sticking out of a skinny brown book of poems on the end of the shelf. The paper was stained and shredded in places, so I unfolded it carefully. *The Aidenn Chronicle* was printed across the top and the date was July 9, 1966. The headline read, "Isaac Chambers Arrested on Suspicion of Treason," and there was a black-and-white photo of an angry-looking man with a mustache. It didn't surprise me that this creepy place had always been filled with scary people.

I looked around the room for something else to do, but we'd run out of furniture to snoop through. An oval mirror, yellowed and spotted, hung loosely on the far wall. My reflection looked distorted, as if it were me from another time, like my dad's old childhood photos.

"What are we going to do here?" I asked Mr. Little. He didn't look as if he knew the answer either.

CHAPTER EIGHT

Mr. Little and I ended up spending the next twenty-four hours either on the bed listening for unusual noises or sitting by the window keeping an eye out for more weird people running around the property. At one point I did notice a twinkling light flashing through the trees, but it stopped as soon as the wind died down. We didn't hear anything particularly interesting other than occasional voices downstairs or the screen door slamming shut. And the only signs of life were chipmunks and birds moving around outside.

Tess continued to deliver all my meals on a tray. She never asked why I was refusing to leave my room, and, in fact, didn't seem to care. When I wanted to know if I could have cereal and bananas for breakfast instead of tasteless oatmeal, she claimed that was all they had. When I asked if they had a set of cards, Tess said she was too busy to look, but that I was welcome to hunt around downstairs in the den. And when I worried about the gunshots in the distance that night, she smiled and reminded me it was the Fourth of July . . . that I was hearing the local fireworks.

That was my lowest point, because it felt as if the world was going on without me. And the Fourth of July was normally one of my favorite holidays, because that meant it was summer and I didn't have to please my teachers or my parents or anyone other than myself.

Early the next morning, my second full day on Beyond, I was still sound asleep when someone twisted my big toe through the heavy quilt.

"OW!"

A boy stood at the end of the bed. He looked about my age, although he was smaller than I was. His brown T-shirt had a hole in the shoulder.

"Who are you?" I gasped.

He leaned slowly to the left. "Solo."

I had never heard of anyone in real life named

Solo. We stared at each other. His eyes were green and his skin was a deep golden the way it might be at the end of the summer, not the beginning. He brushed his long, wispy brown hair out of his eyes as he glanced down at my plaid pajama top. I pulled the quilt up to my chin.

"What do you want?" I asked.

"You have to eat breakfast in the kitchen."

I thought about this for a second. "Did Tess say that?"

He shrugged and said, "I'll be down at the dock."

And with that, he turned and ran out of the room.

It was strange, but as soon as he left I felt like I had to follow him. I don't know if it had to do with being trapped in that room for almost two days and finally seeing someone new, but I couldn't stop myself.

Since it was so early and still chilly, I slipped on jeans and a sweatshirt over another shirt and hurried down the stairs. In the large room full of old, smelly books, Aunt Lenore was sitting in a rocking chair by the crackling fireplace, bundled up in blankets. I had almost forgotten that she lived here, since I hadn't seen her except when we arrived. I paused, not sure if it was against the rules for me to run around indoors.

She turned her head slowly, but her eyes were still closed, so I couldn't tell if she was sleeping. Something about Aunt Lenore made every hair on my body stand on end. She probably had no idea who I was or that I had been hiding upstairs in her house.

Silently, I backed out of the room without disturbing her and found Tess in the kitchen. She was peeling potatoes over a large plastic bin filled with food scraps.

"Well, look who's up and about! Decided to have breakfast down here with me today?"

Standing there in the doorway, I suddenly felt self-conscious and regretted leaving my bedroom. I scanned the kitchen. Everything was old-fashioned the way it is in those black-and-white movies my mom watches every Christmas. The refrigerator was a weird smooth white and matched the small oven and the countertops. The sink was huge and had knobs on either side of the faucet. As far as I could tell, there was no microwave or dishwasher or any normal appliances.

"Some boy told me I had to eat in the kitchen."

She paused in the middle of peeling. "He did, did he?"

Then she turned back to the bin.

"I thought you said there weren't any kids around here."

"No," she said, peeling again, "I said there were no appropriate playmates. That would include Samuel."

"He said his name is Solo."

She placed the skinned white potato in a large pot and wiped her hands on a towel. "The only thing you need to know about Samuel is that you can't believe most of what comes out of that boy's mouth. He lives in his own world."

"Is he your son?"

"Heavens, no. I don't have any children."

"Then whose kid is he? Is he related to Aunt Lenore?"

"No, although lately it seems she's better at recognizing him than her own family members. Goodness, Martin, so many questions! Why don't you sit and wait at the table while I make your oatmeal. It'll only take a few minutes to cook."

The heavy metal chair felt cold right through my clothes.

"How do I get to the dock?"

Tess turned and chuckled. She held up a wooden spoon covered in mush.

"You haven't set foot out of your bedroom for two days and nights, except to take a wee, and now you suddenly want a tour of the property at seven in the morning?"

"*Teesssss?*" Aunt Lenore's croaky voice called from the other room. Like a ghost. I shuddered. "My pot of tea is cold!"

"One second!" Tess called back and rolled her eyes. "It's a wonder that woman doesn't float away from all the tea she drinks. Can you go in and get her pot, Martin, while I heat the water?"

My throat tightened. "Do I have to?"

Tess crossed her arms. "She won't bite you."

As I slipped into the warm room, I saw that Aunt Lenore's eyes were closed, her head tilted back against the rocking chair. The blankets had fallen from her shoulders so that I could see her pale blue bathrobe. I silently lifted the flowery teapot and almost got away without waking her, but a wild squawking noise startled us both.

"Is that you, Poe?" she mumbled, and turned her head almost past her shoulder like an owl in a scary movie. Those big bulging eyes of hers studied me.

"It's me, Martin."

She rubbed her forehead and frowned. "Are you stealing my tea?"

I took a step backward. "Tess asked me to get it."

She swiveled her head again, as if searching for other invaders. "Where's Poe?"

I froze, having no idea who she was talking about.

She rocked forward and croaked, "You must have scared him away."

Right then I saw it again—a shadowy blur zooming past a window at the back of the room. Shivers rushed up my spine. I turned and raced down the hall, dropping the pot on the counter next to the steaming kettle. This house had to be the creepiest place on earth.

"Careful!" said Tess. "That porcelain is older than you and me combined."

"I'm not bringing it back," I said and returned to the same chair, wedging myself against the kitchen table. "She definitely doesn't like me."

Tess lifted the tiny white lid and filled the teapot with hot water. "Don't be ridiculous. Lenore just needs to get to know you better." She turned toward the stove and gave the oatmeal a stir. "Help yourself to a glass of milk from the fridge while I check on her."

But as soon as Tess left the kitchen, I slipped out the back screen door and down a path through the woods to find that kid, whatever his name was.

I reminded myself this was an island, so it wasn't like I could get too lost. After winding between pine trees, the path looped around to the same trail Dad and I had followed from the lake up to the house. Somehow everything looked different now, not as creepy from the outside. Tiny purple flowers bloomed along the path and birds chirped in the trees. Up ahead I saw the far end of the dock and hurried down. But the boy wasn't there.

I walked to the end—carefully, so I wouldn't lose my balance—then gazed across the wavy, dark water. Lake Nevermore. What a weird name for a lake. I glanced up at the sky, which was bright blue except for a few puffy clouds drifting over the large mountains in the distance, and I took a deep breath. Dad was right: the air smelled better here, cleaner and sweeter. It wasn't so bad standing outside in the warm sunshine, especially compared to that gloomy house.

Just then a pebble stung the side of my leg.

"Ow!" I cried and whipped around.

There he was, crouched barefoot on a rock

holding a fishing pole, his baggy jeans rolled up to his knees.

"Did you shoot something at me?" I called over.

He didn't say anything. He didn't even look in my direction. I quickly crept down the tipsy dock and climbed through the brush to where he was sitting.

"Watch out for snakes," he said. "They lay their eggs in this area."

Instantly I jumped back, and the boy burst out laughing.

"Oh. You're joking, right?" I asked.

"That was the funniest thing I've ever seen," he said as soon as he caught his breath. "You're even funnier than Clam."

I crouched down next to him. "Are there really snakes around here?"

"I wish," he said, "but there's nothing exciting on Beyond. You have to go to the mainland to run into anything dangerous, like a bear or a bull moose."

Then he raised his fishing pole, wound the handle on the side, and shot the string far out into the lake, creating a high-pitched whirring sound. After that, he froze as if listening for the fish to come. His arms were long and reddish gold, the color of cinnamon.

"Do you like dangerous animals?" I whispered. No response. He stuck out his tongue as he concentrated.

"Who's Clam?"

Something jumped in the water and the boy stood up.

"Got one!"

"A fish?"

"Of course it's a fish. Feels like a bass."

I watched as he pulled back and forth against the bending rod, the tight line flickering in the sunlight. Suddenly, the line went limp.

"Lost him."

"Oh. Sorry about that," I said, unsure how to respond since I had never watched someone fish before.

"So I see you've officially met each other!" Tess called over from the dock. Her arms were crossed and she was frowning. "I suppose it couldn't be avoided."

"We're fishing," I replied.

"Well, your father's on the phone. Said something about checking in?"

I glanced at the boy, who began packing up his stuff like he was late for an appointment and had to leave.

"Can you tell him I'll call back in a few minutes? I'm kinda busy right now."

CHAPTER NINE

I followed Solo through the woods to another part of the island where a long pointy green boat was tied to a tree stump near the water. He untied it and shoved it into the lake.

"Is that your rowboat?"

"It's a canoe."

"What's the difference between a rowboat and a canoe?"

He shrugged. "One's a rowboat and the other's a canoe."

He climbed in and sat on the back bench.

"Where're you going?" I asked.

"Other side of the lake to meet some friends."

"Are you rowing there?"

"I'm *paddling* there. This is a paddle."

I watched as he arranged his metal box and pole like he was an expert fisherman—or paddleman— about to set off on an adventure. I didn't understand what had come over me, but more than anything I wanted to get to know this kid. I had never met anyone like him.

"Can I come?" I asked, surprising myself because I had no interest in going anywhere in a wobbly boat.

He paused as if actually considering it. "Do you like to jump?"

Immediately, I squatted to the ground and jumped as high as I could.

His mouth dropped open and he laughed again. His laugh was loud and strong.

"Do you do that stuff on purpose?"

I was confused. "What stuff?"

The boy picked up the paddle without answering and pushed against the mud on the bottom of the lake.

"Wait," I said, stepping into the water. "Are you coming back?"

"Depends," he replied as the boat floated backward.

"On what?"

"Whether or not I survive jumping off Pluto's Cliff. It's a good twenty feet above the lake."

What was he talking about? "Why would you jump off a cliff?"

"Why wouldn't you?" he replied as he turned the boat and paddled forward. "It's the best feeling in the whole world—*unless* . . . "

"Unless what?"

Now he was so far out in the water we practically had to yell.

"—unless you miss the sweet spot and *SPLAT!*"

And with that, the mysterious boy and his canoe disappeared around the bend.

I ran along the shore, hurdling over the sharp twiggy bushes, tripping against roots and rocks to catch a glimpse of him, but he was gone. And the island was silent again.

As I wandered up the path toward the house, I tried imagining how it would feel to jump off the side of a cliff into ice-cold water. But even thinking about the rocky ledge made me queasy.

"Well, there you are," said Tess. "Your oatmeal is almost ruined from sitting on the stove so long."

"I'm not really hungry," I replied, swatting a mosquito that had followed me into the kitchen. I slumped down at the table and asked, "Have you ever jumped off Pluto's Cliff?"

The corners of her mouth curled slightly. "Not in forty years. Besides, jumping off the cliffs is prohibited nowadays."

"You mean it's against the law?"

"Well, it should be, so stop talking to Samuel and letting him fill your head with crazy ideas. Your parents are going to want you in one piece at the end of the month."

There was no way I was staying on this island for a whole month. That's when I remembered my father had called.

"What did my dad say?"

Tess filled a huge pot with water and placed it on the stove. "That he would be busy most of the morning but would call again in the afternoon."

Outside, the wind picked up, which made the screen door open and close all on its own. The windows rattled too. Everything about this house gave me the heebie-jeebies.

"Where does that kid live?"

"That," said Tess, shaking her head, "is what we call a loaded question." She turned the flame up under the pot and then faced me, her hands on her hips. "Martin, try not to get too mixed up with Samuel."

"Why not?"

"Because he's *wild*," she said quietly.

"What do you mean?"

"A wild child's made from trouble, and that's all you need to know."

The last thing that interested me was anything to do with trouble, and I would never break the law. I loved rules the way I loved orderly Martinville and perfectly sliced bananas on my cereal every day.

"But he seems nice," I mumbled.

"For goodness' sake, you just met him. How can you know if he's nice or not?"

I didn't have an answer to that. But I did know that I'd liked him the minute I saw him. In fact, it was a stronger feeling than liking. I wanted to follow him. And watch him. And talk to him. I had so many questions, even more than usual.

It's not as if I'd never had a close friend before. For a long time I did everything with Jayla Curry. She was allowed to ride her scooter anywhere she wanted, so we hung out in my basement and played video games all the time. I even showed her Martinville and she liked it. But at some point last winter, Jayla and a lot of her friends started acting dumb, doing fancy things with their hair and talking about their clothes and giggling all the time at stupid stuff. And then one day, when we were in the middle of playing Retaliating Robots in my basement, she leaned over and kissed my face.

"Gross!" I yelled and rubbed it off.

Jayla glared at me and then ran up the basement stairs like the house was on fire. The whole thing was really annoying. And super gross. We've avoided each other ever since.

But this feeling was different. I couldn't think of any friend I had ever thought about the way I was thinking about this kid. Maybe it had to do with being trapped in that bedroom. Or maybe I was under some spell on this spooky island.

Suddenly the door in the back hall burst open. Aunt Lenore appeared, wearing a long gray dress. The mound of blue-white fluff on her head was sticking straight up in the air like she had been electrocuted.

"What on earth is taking so long, Tess?" she snapped. "I can't find my sapphire ring anywhere. I'll be late for the garden party. "

"Settle down," said Tess. "You'll scare Martin."

I had never seen a real witch, but that's exactly

what I thought of when I saw that old woman teetering in the doorway.

Aunt Lenore turned toward me and stared directly into my eyes. "That child isn't Samuel," she said.

"No, it's not," said Tess. "Remember, this is Martin? Martin Hart."

"Oh yes." She frowned. "The boy who stole my tea."

I glanced at Tess, who rolled her eyes and said, "Martin is here to lend a hand this summer. We need the help."

What was she talking about now? Dad hadn't mentioned anything about having to work. I was too young to work.

Aunt Lenore continued to glare at me suspiciously and then asked, "Is he the one you hired to paint the house?"

"Exactly," said Tess, "and I'm sure he'll do a fine job. Now go back to your bedroom and close the door. I'll be right with you."

"What's she talking about?" I whispered nervously as soon as the witch disappeared. "I don't know how to paint a house!"

"Of course you don't, but in case you haven't

noticed, Lenore's not too connected to reality at the moment. I'm guessing she'll forget that whole conversation in half an hour. But it's important to let her think she's in charge—at least until we know more from the doctor. Anyway, I do have a few daily chores I'll start you on now that you've decided to join the world again."

Chores?

"I should really call my dad first. Do you have a phone I could use?"

"I already told you, your father said he would call later. And you need to eat something," she said as she slipped a bowl of pasty oatmeal and a brown jug in front of me. "Try it with maple syrup this time. It'll taste better. Now I have to get your great-aunt ready, and then we can make plans for you, young man."

CHAPTER TEN

I didn't like the sound of that word, *plans*. My only plan for the future was to get off this island as soon as possible and get back to Delaware. All at once I felt the need to call Mom right away, as if it were a real emergency. What was I thinking, agreeing to stay practically a whole week in this house?

I searched the kitchen and found a black landline phone in the corner by a spice rack. But it wasn't a normal phone. It was the old-fashioned kind with a circle in the middle and ten holes. I tried dialing Mom's number by pressing and moving the holes, but I got nothing other than a fuzzy dial tone.

"Well, look at you! You must be Jonny's boy?"

I spun around. An old man wearing overalls, a

yellow shirt, and black boots stood in the doorway. He had a potbelly and thick white stubble all over his face and neck, but something about his outfit and his expression made him look like a giant three-year-old boy.

"You're the spitting image of Jonny when he was your age," he added, smiling.

I still didn't say anything. No one had ever told me I looked like my father.

"I'm Ned. *Uncle* Ned."

"Oh. Hi."

So this was the uncle my dad didn't like. Other than his resemblance to an enormous toddler, I couldn't tell what was supposed to be wrong with him. But I didn't think it was polite to stare too much, so I returned to the phone and poked at it some more.

"Do you need help with something?" Uncle Ned asked.

Without looking at him I replied, "I don't know how to make this work."

He stepped a little closer and stretched his body cautiously as if leaning over a deep hole.

"The telephone? You don't know how to work a telephone?"

He took off his dirty cap with the words "ONLY the Best" printed on the front and scratched his curly gray hair. It was flattened against his head like a helmet.

"I know how to use a normal phone," I mumbled, feeling embarrassed, since usually I could figure out how to work anything.

"Well then, dial it like a normal phone," he said. "Is that porridge and syrup on the table?"

I nodded.

"Can I have it or you gonna eat it?"

"You can have it."

The old man wiped his hands up and down the front of his overalls.

"I don't want to have to take off my work boots, but the ladies will have a fit if I tromp across the floor. Can you bring the bowl over here? And pour on a heap of syrup first, if you don't mind."

Before I could move, Tess stepped out of Aunt Lenore's bedroom door and into the hallway.

"What's going on now?" she asked as she walked toward us. "Are you looking for something, Ned?"

He lowered his eyes and his voice as if he were in trouble. "Jonny's boy said I could have that bowl of porridge."

"You already ate a full plate of eggs this morning," said Tess. "I'm not running a restaurant here! Now scoot from my kitchen and get some of those projects done before this island falls apart."

Ned hung his head like a scolded dog and backed out the screen door. I felt a little sorry for him, even though he was kind of weird.

"And you," she said to me, "get away from that telephone and eat your breakfast. You're much too thin to be giving away your meals."

From her tone, I knew I had to do what she said. So I returned to the table and forced myself to swallow each gloppy bite, like it would be my last. Meanwhile Tess dropped glass jars in the pot of boiling water. Why would anyone cook jars? Almost nothing about this place was normal.

"As soon as you're finished, go outside while I put up some rhubarb preserves. I'm way behind here. We'll make those plans for you later, after lunch."

"But what am I supposed to do outside?"

Tess turned around and frowned.

"For goodness' sake, Martin, do what children your age have been doing since the beginning of time. Explore!"

I had been a little curious about that twinkling light I saw in a clearing through the trees from my bedroom window. So I ventured carefully into the woods to look for it, keeping an eye out for anything dangerous, like that dark shadow sneaking around the island, or snake eggs.

I'd hoped the clearing would be a sunny meadow full of clover and flowers. Instead, the ground was covered in flat gray rocks and dark moss. Giant mushrooms grew in damp cracks. And over on the far edge stood a bizarre sculpture made of metal, almost as tall as the trees. Parts of it reminded me of wings, and other parts looked like legs. Several thin blades sparkled as they spun slowly in the breeze like miniature windmills. I had never seen anything like it. It was weird and random but, at the same time, kind of interesting.

All at once I had an urge to build, and since I had nothing else to do I gathered supplies: stones, leaves, sticks, vines, pine needles. The sun was higher in the sky now, and it was getting hot. I took off my sweatshirt and placed Mr. Little on guard on a nearby stump so I could concentrate.

A couple of hours must have passed by the time I heard the boy's voice call from somewhere nearby.

"What are you doing?"

I shielded my eyes and glanced around but couldn't see him. Then a shadow blinked across the sun and I saw the outline of his body. He was bouncing on top of the highest tree, like he was riding a horse.

I stood up and gasped, "Be careful!"

The bouncing shadow stopped.

"Why? Is a branch gonna bite me?" he said and laughed carelessly.

Tess was right. This kid was trouble. It made me nervous to see him way up there, so I bent down to continue working. The town square and main roads were basically complete, so now I could begin construction outward starting with the post office. Papery bark from the white trees made decent walls and I could use leaves for the roof.

Minutes later, a dirty foot slid past me and almost knocked over the gazebo by the duck pond on the village square.

"What's all this?"

He crouched down and I couldn't help studying his face, inches from mine. His eyes were as green as the moss.

"It's a town."

He inspected what I had created so far. "Why?"

"Why what?"

"Why are you making it?"

I had never thought about *why* I did anything. I just did it. "It's something I like to do."

The boy stood up and crossed his arms. "Where's the jail? And the dump? And the graveyard?"

I placed a large pinecone, as a mailbox, next to the post office. "It's not that kind of town."

"What do you mean? Every town has those things. Every real town."

"It's not a real town."

I didn't say that to make him laugh, but he cracked up anyway. "You're hilarious, Martian."

"What did you call me?" I stood up next to him and brushed off my pants. "My name is Martin."

"I know, but *Martian*," he replied firmly, "is a way better name for you."

It occurred to me I hadn't told him my name before. I wondered if he knew anything else about me. And if so, who would have told him?

"And your name is Samuel?" I said.

"I already told you," he corrected me, "it's Solo." Then he opened his fist and asked, "What's this?"

I had forgotten about Mr. Little. I grabbed him

and shoved him in my pocket, then bent down in embarrassment and continued to build. Solo sat down and watched me quietly for a few minutes, the way you would observe an animal in a zoo.

"When you're all done with that, Martian, wanna swim over to Only's and get some day-olds?"

I had no idea what he was talking about, but it didn't matter. "I can't swim," I said.

He scrunched up his face. "What do you mean? Everyone can swim."

"My dad made me take lessons one summer, but it turns out I can't float," I explained. "And if you can't float, you can't swim."

"Says who?"

"My dad."

"Well, Clam—who's really small and sinks like an anchor—can swim from here to Prophet's Beach without stopping."

I didn't know what to say. I guess I didn't know why I couldn't swim. Or fish or climb a tree or anything normal boys could do, feats even some little kid named Clam had accomplished.

"I should hang around here anyway," I mumbled and brushed the dirt and pine needles off my hands. "My dad's calling back any minute."

Solo stood up. "What for?"

"Just checking in, but he'll probably want to come get me soon."

He grabbed a few rocks from my pile of supplies and threw one into the woods. "Aren't you staying?"

For some reason, my throat grew tight. Did he want me to stay? I stood up next to him. "Nah, I was just trying it out for the week, but . . ."

He studied me, waiting for me to finish my sentence.

"But my mom really needs me at home. She's not used to being alone all day, having no one to take care of and all that. You know how needy moms are."

"Not really," he replied as he turned and threw another rock.

I wanted to ask him a million questions, like where he lived and who Clam was and why Tess said he was trouble.

"So when are you leaving?"

Another rock flew from his hand.

"I don't know—in a couple of days. Or maybe not until Saturday. It depends on when my parents get here."

The idea of staying in that strange house one more night sent chills up my spine, but leaving without getting to know Solo somehow felt worse.

The last rock went the farthest as it sailed through the air and hit the metal sculpture.

In the distance, I heard a phone ring.

"I bet that's for me," I said, starting to run. "Wait here, I'll be right back."

CHAPTER ELEVEN

Tess stood outside the kitchen stretching the long curly phone cord out the back door as I rushed down the path.

"Here he is, Mr. Hart," she said cheerfully and then whispered to me, "It's your father again, and by the way, your lunch has been waiting for you in the dining room."

How was I supposed to know that? And where was the dining room? Grown-ups never told you anything, but they expected you to know everything.

"Hi, Dad."

"Hey, buddy! From what Tess has told me, it sounds like you're settling in nicely."

"Uh—"

"I'm glad to hear it. I knew you'd be fine."

"But Dad, I—"

"Can't talk long! Crazy-busy day at the office."

"But wait, my cell phone is— "

"Oh, and Mom's having car troubles. Again. The minivan's gonna be out of commission for a while, so we're operating on one car for the next couple of weeks."

Panic swelled throughout my body. Mom *promised* to come get me in exactly six days. I mean, it was true that I was feeling a little torn about leaving right away, but I definitely didn't want to stay more than a couple extra days, just to get to know Solo a little bit.

"I've got another call coming in. Remember— put your best foot forward! Mom sends her love."

"But—"

The phone went dead and the room began to spin. I was sweating in places I didn't know could sweat.

Here I was, potentially trapped for the entire month of July in a spooky house with a bunch of old people on a remote island in the middle of a huge, cold lake with no possibility of even running away, all because I couldn't swim or row a boat—or even use the phone! I didn't have a best foot to put forward. Neither of my feet worked.

At that moment, the shadow zoomed past the kitchen window. I rushed over and peered through the dirty glass. It was that same mystery person— the one I had seen from my bedroom that first day, scurrying through the trees in dark clothes. I took a deep breath and decided to find out once and for all what was going on here. Maybe if I could prove to my dad that this place wasn't safe, he would have a reason to rescue me.

By the time I'd raced outside, I barely caught a glimpse of the mystery person's black hood as he zigzagged through the woods and down the hill toward the water. He wasn't using the path, so I tried to follow him directly through the thick bushes and scratchy weeds, making as little noise as possible. Low branches stabbed my face and arms as if the trees were trying to hold me back.

Finally, I saw a dark figure in the distance leaning against a large boulder by the lake. Obviously, he couldn't go farther unless he swam, so I crept slowly toward him to get a better idea of the situation. But it turned out it wasn't a person at all. It was a black bird perched on the highest point of the rock. As soon as it heard me, the bird spread his large black wings and flew off over the trees.

I had ended up where I started out that morning, at the rock where Solo was fishing. I walked along the shore over to the dock and out to the end so I could get a fuller view of the island. But I saw nothing and no one. Just trees. The lake was very still now, as if it had swallowed the secret trespasser.

I stretched out across the hard wooden planks, covered my face, and moaned. What I needed was my own plan. I considered returning to my bedroom and willing myself into a coma for the rest of the month, but that didn't seem realistic. What was it that people did when they were marooned on an island? I think it was wave a white flag to nearby ships or low-flying airplanes, neither of which seemed to pass by Lake Nevermore . . . located in the middle of nowhere.

Then a huge splash startled me. I sat up and scanned the water, but I saw only a circle of ripples. Whatever it was, it had gone back under. It probably couldn't be that little person, since he was wearing lots of clothes. I thought of those horrible creatures that lurked in lakes and that might or might not be real, like the Loch Ness Monster. I didn't know what to do. Should I stay still? Or run? Before I could decide, a familiar shape shot up out of the water.

"Solo?!"

He disappeared back into the lake. I waited and waited. How long could he hold his breath? I began to worry and stood up.

"*SOLO?*"

Next thing I knew, a wall of water hit my back.

"Hey!" I yelled. "What did you do that for?"

By then he had vanished under the dock. I bent down to peer through the cracks. Water dribbled down my face and through my eyes, making it difficult to see the shadow moving beneath me.

"What did your dad say?" he asked, his voice echoing under the wooden planks. "Are you leaving in a couple days?"

Now I could see the outline of his head bobbing on the surface.

"Nope. Maybe next week."

Seconds later, he emerged into the daylight and swam over to the ladder, resting his bare arms on the top rung.

"Then you can come to the roast if you want."

I sat up and squeezed water out of my damp shirt. "The what?"

"Me and my friends get together sometimes and roast stuff over a fire pit."

Roast stuff? Fire pit? Normally, I would turn down that kind of invitation without hesitating. For one thing, if it involved a group of boys who were used to messing around outdoors, I wouldn't fit in at all. And then there was the part about those wild boys building a huge fire that could easily burn out of control and kill us . . . But on the other hand, there was something about Solo that made me want to find out more. And obviously he had survived previous roasts.

"Where is it?" I asked.

"Prophet's Beach by the old campground." He pointed across the lake, as if that made any difference to me. "It's been closed down for years, so no one else uses it."

This was sounding less and less appealing, but still . . .

"How would I get there?"

"I'll pick you up."

"In a boat?"

"What else? A truck?"

I wasn't sure about this. It definitely sounded like trouble. "I should ask Tess first."

"Don't!" he said, suddenly standing halfway up the ladder. "You can't ever tell anyone."

I couldn't stop staring at him. He reminded me of an exotic animal. Like a leopard or panther or one of those other safari cats you see on nature shows. It was the way his long tanned neck and bare stomach tensed up, ready to spring at his prey. Was that why Tess called him wild?

"What do you mean I can't tell anyone? I can't just leave, can I?"

"Geez, Martian," he said as he pushed himself away from the dock. "All you ever do is ask questions."

CHAPTER TWELVE

As Solo swam away he called out something about needing to find "day-olds" for lunch—whatever those were—and that's when I realized I was starving. I'd had nothing to eat except that crummy oatmeal hours ago.

Tess had said my lunch was waiting on the dining room table, so I walked back up the dirt trail toward the front porch. Most likely it would be a boring bowl of soup and a slice of toast, which was what she'd given me for lunch the day before in my bedroom.

I remembered seeing a long table in a fancy room near the front entrance when Dad and I first walked through the house, so I figured that had to be the dining room. Before climbing the front steps, I stopped to read the strange sign again, *The Great and Beautiful Be*. The *yond* must have fallen off a long time ago, because the broken edge was smooth and gray.

I had an urge to ring the melon-sized bell by the door, but the house seemed unusually quiet inside. The door creaked softly as I entered the front hall and listened. Not a sound. I assumed since they were all old people they were probably taking naps like my grampy used to do whenever he visited us.

When I crept into the dining room, I was shocked to see a black bird, just like the one on the rock, standing on top of the table and eating off a plate.

"Gah! SHOO!"

The bird bounced down to the floor and around the corner toward the hall just as Tess rushed into the room from the opposite side.

"What's wrong?" she asked, drying her hands on a towel.

"A *bird* ate my lunch!"

She frowned and replied, "That wasn't your lunch. Lunchtime is over."

"But I'm hungry."

"Well then, next time don't let your meal sit out until it spoils. You can wait for dinner."

I couldn't believe what I was hearing.

"But my mom lets me eat whenever I'm hungry."

"Do I look like your mother?" she asked in a high voice. "Now where did Poe go?"

"Who?"

"The raven, Lenore's bird."

I pointed toward the hallway, and Tess followed its trail. By now I was so hungry I didn't even wonder why a creepy black bird was allowed to bounce freely around the house. Honestly, hardly anything could surprise me anymore about this place.

My empty stomach forced me to desperate measures. I decided to hunt for some of those blueberries Dad had pointed out along the path. Less than ten feet from the house, I found bushes covered in them. I carried a handful down to the edge of the lake to rinse off and, for a moment, felt proud of my survival skills. But as soon as I popped a wet one in my mouth I gagged. It was way too tart, nothing like the ones from the grocery store. I forced myself to swallow but then chucked the rest of the berries in the lake. Now my stomach growled even more loudly, like it was mad at me.

Dad was right. I wasn't a normal boy. I couldn't even manage to eat stupid berries. I reached into my pocket for Mr. Little to console myself, but he wasn't there. I jumped up and checked all my pockets. He was gone!

"*Mr. Little?!*" I yelled before realizing that wouldn't make a difference.

Think. Think. Where was he last? The town!

As fast as I could, I tore back to the clearing and bent down in front of the miniature village. There he was, floating on his back in the duck pond. Wet but safe. I picked up his tiny gray body and dried him against the front of my jeans since my shirt was still damp.

"How did you end up in the water?" I asked into his teeny ear. "Are you okay?"

I held him against my cheek.

"At least you know how to float on your back. Otherwise, you could've drowned."

"Hello again!"

Uncle Ned was standing on a ladder behind the tall metal statue.

"Who're you talking to over there?" he asked.

"No one," I called and slipped damp Mr. Little deep into my pocket.

I walked across the rocks and moss and stared up at the strange metal shape.

"Did you make that?" I asked.

"Nope," he replied as he tightened a screw in the middle of a spinning piece. "A friend did. Just giving it a tune-up."

The wind picked up, causing various parts to turn and twirl, as if it were coming alive.

"What's it supposed to be?"

Several seconds passed before Uncle Ned answered.

"I don't know that it's supposed to be anything in particular," he said and switched tools.

"I think it looks like two giant roosters fighting, or maybe turkeys."

That made him chuckle, followed by a long sigh.

"You may be on to something there," he said as he climbed down, unlatched the top of the ladder, and folded it in half in one smooth motion.

"Does it do anything?"

"Like what?"

"Like make music in the wind," I replied, "or spray water in the air?"

The old man squinted at me, then at the sculpture.

"Not that I know of, though it does cast a lovely

shadow, especially in the fall."

I didn't really get the point of a contraption that didn't do anything.

"But I like the way you think," he said and smiled. "Do you play backgammon?"

"What's that?"

"A game of skill and luck, just like life."

"That sounds like a lot of games."

"Ha! I guess so. You've never heard of backgammon?"

I shook my head.

"Well then, how about checkers?"

"I've heard of it. But I've never actually played it."

"Everybody's played checkers."

I shook my head. "Not me."

"Imagine that. How old are you?"

"Eleven."

"What do you like to play, then?"

"World Warriors, Destruction Down Under, Mutant Minnows, stuff like that."

He scrunched up his eyebrows and curled his mouth like he'd never heard of video games. Then he hoisted the ladder onto his left shoulder.

"Listen," he said, pausing to glimpse over at the woods as if he was expecting someone. "I'm gonna be gone for a few days, but I want you to stop by my cabin when I get back. We'll get to know each other a little better."

I didn't know what to think of Uncle Ned. That morning in the kitchen I'd thought he was odd, but now he seemed, well, sort of interesting. No one had ever told me they liked the way I think, and I wondered what he meant by that. Dad had acted as if something was wrong with him, but maybe it was a disease he had a long time ago and now it was gone.

As soon as Uncle Ned marched off into the woods, carrying the ladder and a belt full of tools, I realized I was not only starving, but also exhausted, and for once in my life a nap seemed like a good idea.

Except for the faint sound of old scratchy music in another room, the house was still quiet, so Mr. Little and I sneaked up the stairs to my bedroom. I was in no mood to bump into anyone else, especially not scary Aunt Lenore. Before lying down, I changed out of my damp shirt and searched through my suitcase for another one. Tucked between my clothes, I found a bulging yellow envelope I hadn't noticed before. It was a package stuffed with snacks! My favorite granola bars, peanut butter cookies, a bag of gummy bears, a candy bar . . . and a note:

Dear Martin,

I know this may not have been the way you hoped to spend the summer, sweetheart, but try to enjoy yourself. I thought you'd like a few goodies—please don't eat them all at once.
Love, Mom

It was very short and said nothing about picking me up in six days. And if she knew this wasn't the way I would choose to spend the summer, not in a million years, then how could I possibly enjoy myself?

But for the moment I didn't really care, because I was ecstatic about all the treats. I lay back on my bed and, ignoring my mother's suggestion, downed the entire supply. She probably would have approved if she knew they were starving me here.

A breeze blew through the open window. Birds chirped in the trees. My eyes started to get heavy as I thought about Solo's invitation to hang out with his friends, and the more I thought about it, the more I sort of liked the idea. I mean, if I had to be trapped on this dumb island for a while, it would be nice to meet a few kids so I wouldn't die of boredom. Soon I was imagining a scene where Solo and I were standing in the center of a crowd of wild boys like him, who were all listening to me tell stories that were so funny they couldn't stop laughing . . . and then before I knew it, I was fast asleep.

Two hours later I puked for the third time into the crooked toilet in the crooked bathroom.

"Tell me again what you ate from your suitcase!"

Tess stood over me holding towels.

"What I already told you," I cried, "stuff I eat all the time at home!"

My whole body shook. Beads of sweat rolled down my face.

"How were you feeling this morning?"

"Fine," I managed to moan just before I barfed again.

Tess ran a small cloth under the faucet and wiped my face.

"I don't understand," she said, "this came out of nowhere?"

"*Maybe* if I'd had lunch, it wouldn't have *happened!*"

She rinsed the towel again and spread it over the back of my neck. The coolness helped a little.

"A big lunch would have made it worse. You

must have a bug. Unless—did Samuel give you any-thing unusual to eat? Maybe something he found?"

That's when I remembered.

"I did pick some blueberries."

"What blueberries?" she asked sternly.

"By the house, along the path to the dock. My dad said they might be blueberries."

"You ate those?"

"Just one. I washed it in the lake first."

"Oh, Martin," she said and slumped down next to me, "those aren't blueberries. Never, *ever* eat anything you find outside. Lots of things out in the forest, especially berries, could make you much sicker than this if you don't know what they are. The same with the lake water—you aren't supposed to drink it. And if Samuel ever again tries to convince you to—"

"It wasn't him! I ate the stupid berry on my own," I said, my bottom lip quivering. "I was starving and you wouldn't feed me! AND I DON'T KNOW ANYTHING! I don't how to swim or row a boat or climb a tree or fish or play checkers or even use that old stupid phone!"

Right then I burst into tears. Everything that had built up inside of me since the beginning of the week poured out.

A few seconds later Tess held a glass of water under my nose. "Small sips, they'll help." I was in no position to argue, so between sobs I managed to swallow a little bit of water.

"Listen," she said, putting her arm around my shoulders. "I'm not used to having children in the house. I admit I may be a little rigid in my ways. But you need to pay attention if you don't want to run into trouble around here. All right?"

I sniffled and nodded, but not too hard because I didn't want to throw up again.

"Let's meet halfway," she continued. "If you want to stay outside and play through lunch, just let me know. And if you miss a meal, you can get something for yourself, like toast with peanut butter and honey. How does that sound?"

The mention of food made me puke one last time. But after that I felt better. "Okay," I said shakily. Even if I did have to live off toast for the rest of the month, it was a huge relief to know I wasn't going to keel over and die on Beyond Island.

CHAPTER THIRTEEN

I slept all the way to nine o'clock the next morning and probably would have slept longer if not for the distant banging that woke me. As soon as I slipped out of bed to take a look, the noise stopped. I opened the window as wide as it would go and stuck my head outside to listen again, but nothing.

"Nice to see you're awake." Tess stood in the doorway holding a tray. "I wasn't sure if you were still feeling under the weather."

"I feel okay," I said after taking a deep breath. "Who's hammering?"

She paused and turned an ear. "I don't hear hammering."

"But it woke me up just now."

"Probably a woodpecker. They can be very loud," she replied and carried the tray back into the hall. "Since you're up, why don't you get dressed and eat this downstairs? It's a lovely morning!"

Luckily, Aunt Lenore was nowhere in sight as I sneaked through the house. Dozens of jars filled with red goop were lined up on the kitchen table where Tess sat, writing on white labels and sticking them onto the jars.

As I poured syrup on my oatmeal, I picked one up. The label read, *Beyond Island Rhubarb Preserves.* "What's this?"

"Jam. Lenore loves it on a raisin scone."

It sounded like more old people food to me. "She's going to eat all this?"

"It lasts the year, and I'll give some to a few folks over on the mainland."

Tess picked up a tiny spoon and dipped it in one of the jars. "Here, try a bite."

To my surprise, I liked it. In fact, I even noticed my oatmeal tasted better this morning.

Just as I was getting to the bottom of my bowl, Solo appeared outside the window pressing his face against the middle pane. He made funny faces and slobbered all over the glass. Immediately my heart began to pound, which was a weird feeling—like if I didn't hurry I would lose him forever. I downed the rest of my oatmeal in one huge bite and popped up from the table.

"Where are you suddenly off to faster than a flea?" asked Tess, following my gaze.

Solo made a crazy face and ducked. I had to force myself not to laugh.

"Um, exploring?"

She raised her eyebrows suspiciously but then smiled.

"Well, have a good time, but don't forget I want you to start some chores today. There's plenty to do around here, and we could use your help. And no eating berries!"

I had never done chores in my life, but I didn't have time to waste complaining. By the time I reached the side of the house, Solo was gone. I crept through the woods whispering his name, but there was no sign of him. Just when I was about to give up and go down to the dock to wait, he jumped out from behind a bush and tackled me to the ground.

"*OW!*"

Straddling my stomach, he held my hands

above my head, grinding them into the dirt. "That was too easy," he said, squeezing my wrists tighter. Pebbles pierced my skin.

"Stop it—it hurts! And I can't breathe."

He perched there another couple of seconds, then rolled off of me.

"Wow, Martian. Even Clam could hold you down with one hand."

I was getting tired of being compared to some kid with a weird name who could supposedly do everything.

"I don't like fighting."

I got up and brushed off my shirt and shorts. It was one of my newer shirts, and I hated getting it dirty.

"We weren't fighting. It was wrestling."

"Wrestling is the same as fighting," I said as I checked the back of my shorts for more dirt.

"No it's not."

It felt the same to me, but I didn't want Solo to get mad and leave, so I changed the subject. "How long have you lived around here anyway?"

Before answering, he jumped straight up in the air, grabbed a branch, and swung his legs back and forth.

"Most of my life."

I leaned against the tree and watched him pull his legs over his head and hang upside down like it was the easiest thing in the world.

"So you must know my aunt Lenore?" I asked his upside-down face.

"Sort of. We used to talk a little when she took walks around the island. But I haven't seen her in a while."

"Have you ever talked to my uncle Ned?"

"Sure."

"What's he like? I don't think my dad likes him, but he seems nice. Is he nice?"

Solo didn't answer. Instead, he flipped backward and dropped down to the ground.

"Ready for tonight?" he asked.

"Tonight?"

"The roast, remember? I'll pick you up later at the dock when the sun is right at the tree line," he said, pointing at the sky.

After the berry disaster the day before and then almost being crushed in a wrestling match a minute ago, I didn't feel felt brave enough to go anymore. But I didn't know how to say that to Solo. He didn't seem to realize that I wasn't good at anything he was good at. He was treating me like I was a friend he'd hung out with for years.

"That gives us the rest of the day to practice," Solo added.

"To practice for the roast?"

"To practice swimming," he said. "I'll teach you."

I wasn't expecting that either.

"I can't. Tess wants me to do chores."

"I heard her," said Solo. "She said 'today,' not now. You can do them later."

"How did you hear her?"

"You can hear everything going on in that house."

"You can? *Everything?*"

All of a sudden I felt completely embarrassed, remembering how I'd puked and yelled and cried like a little kid.

"Come on, Martian," he said, "we'll start with floating. It's easy."

Getting in the freezing water and trying to float was the last thing I wanted to do. A couple of summers ago, swimming lessons at Dad's golf club had been a disaster. I was so bad they took me out of the group lesson and assigned me to my own private instructor. I later overheard him tell Dad that I lacked basic synchronization skills, which sounded awful even though I didn't know what it meant, but I was too afraid to look it up. That's when the lessons stopped. And I could tell Dad was disappointed, because he barely smiled at me for a whole week.

I stared down at the ground. "I just don't want to, okay?"

A leaf floated down from a tree and Solo swatted it so hard it ripped in half. "Then what do you want to do?"

What I really wanted to do was play video games. That was pretty much what I always did with my spare time. Until my brain felt fried and then I watched TV. Sometimes I read *Revengenators* or even a book, but only fun stuff like sci-fi stories about other galaxies. And of course, I liked to play with Martinville, but that was usually at night before bed.

"Do you want to check on the town I built?" I suggested.

He looked down and crossed his arms. "Not really."

Both of us stared at the ground and said nothing. Because there was nothing to say. We had nothing in common.

Then Solo squeezed his lips and sighed.

"See ya later, Martian."

That was exactly what I felt like, a Martian. An alien. A failure on earth.

For the first time in ages, I had the chance to be friends with a boy I liked a lot—more than I'd ever liked anyone—and I was already blowing it.

For the next hour I wandered around the island thinking about what my dad had said: *Do the opposite of what you would normally do.* So I decided I would force myself to meet Solo at the dock that afternoon and go with him in his tipsy boat to an abandoned campground to light things on fire with a crowd of tough boys who illegally jumped off cliffs and would probably hate me the moment they met me.

I practically passed out just thinking about it.

Another complication was Tess. Solo had warned me not to tell her about the secret meeting, but if I got caught it would be smart to have bargaining points. Which meant I should go back to the house and offer to do chores.

"After lunch, you can start with the wood," she said as she dried plates with a dish towel hanging from her apron. "We had a delivery a couple weeks ago, but Ned hasn't had a chance to stack it."

"Stack wood?"

"You won't get it all done in a day, but do what you can."

"But I don't how to stack wood."

"For goodness' sake. Walk across the way over to the woodpile outside the shed, pick up a log and lay it down inside the shed. Repeat in rows until you're done. It's the simplest thing in the world."

I sighed loudly. This was not what I had expected when Tess mentioned chores. I thought I would fold laundry or organize the silverware drawer. Not to mention all the dusting that needed to be done around the house.

"Where's the shed?" I asked.

"I just told you. It's across the way."

"What does that mean? Why can't you just show me where it is?"

Tess placed the stack of dried plates in a cabinet.

"How will you ever learn to solve anything for yourself, Martin, if everyone's always figuring it out for you?"

It seemed like a very inefficient way of getting anything done, letting people struggle and waste time while someone else could easily show them or even tell them in one minute. But I didn't bother to explain that to Tess, since everything around here was done using the slowest, most old-fashioned methods possible. For example, who would go to all that trouble cooking jars and making jam when you could buy jam at the store?

After lunch I stepped outside and looked around for a shed, but I saw no sign of it through the trees. So I wandered over to the clearing where I might have a better view and, at the same time, make a quick stop to work on my town. As I bent over Main Street, I immediately noticed something was different. A road heading away from the post office had been carved through the moss, ending just beyond the grocery store. I knew I hadn't added it, so it could only be Solo.

All at once, a warm feeling washed over me. I'd known he liked it the moment he started asking me questions, but I could also tell it was something he had never thought about before. Maybe that was why he had pretended he didn't want to work on it—because he wanted to surprise me! Right then I decided I would call the town Soloville and would build the perfect place where Solo and I could live together. I'd add a library at the end of Main Street, and a science museum nearby, and there would be a restaurant on every corner.

As I searched for good chunks of bark to make walls for a movie theater, I caught a glimpse of a real roof in the distance past the metal sculpture. The wood shed.

I sighed deeply and forced myself to stop building. There would be plenty of time for that later.

The scruffy bushes scratched my legs as I made my way toward the small wooden shack. It was wedged between two boulders near the edge of the island. The double doors had been left open, and the floor inside was dirt. Next to the shed was a pile of wood so enormous it practically reached the top of the roof. This was my afternoon chore? It would take a year for me to stack all this.

I picked up the first log very carefully, so I wouldn't get a splinter in my hand or dirt on my shirt, and neatly set it inside against the wall. The second log had a gross bug on it, so I had to find a stick to brush it off. But after an hour or so I finally completed two full rows. And the longer I stacked, the more I sort of enjoyed it. Each log fit snugly with the one next to it and above it, like puzzle pieces.

While I worked, I couldn't stop thinking about Solo. He seemed to be the only person who spent time on this island other than Aunt Lenore, Uncle

Ned, and Tess. But he wasn't related to any of them. And yet he seemed to know them all—and they knew he was here, even though he was always sneaking around as if he were trespassing. It made no sense. I couldn't figure out how he was connected to this place.

After a while my body began to feel hot and itchy, so I took a break on one of the boulders and gazed out over the lake. My mind drifted like the leaf I watched float along the top of the water. Everything felt very far away from here, especially Delaware. I wondered if my father would be surprised to see me stacking wood, probably something he and Uncle Jason had loved to do as kids. I assumed Solo stacked wood all the time, and that he could move that mountain of logs in one afternoon. It seemed like there was nothing he couldn't do.

A large dark bird caught my eye as it flew across the sky. That's when I noticed the sun was resting just a few inches above the tallest tree. Almost the time when I was supposed to meet Solo at the dock. A jolt of energy shot through my body—kind of like fear, but mixed with excitement. It was time to go.

CHAPTER FOURTEEN

I didn't want to be late, so I jumped off the rock and raced past Soloville without stopping. Luckily no one seemed to be around when I slipped through the house and hurried upstairs to change into my brown sweatshirt and old jeans, which seemed like the best things to wear to a bonfire at an abandoned campground. I knew I should probably leave Mr. Little behind, but I needed his support.

As soon as I sat down on the dock to wait for Solo, I started thinking about who else would be at the roast. A kid like him probably hung around the toughest boys in all of Maine. The longer I waited, the more I became convinced the whole night would be a disaster—that I wouldn't be able to do anything the other boys did and that I'd completely humiliate myself.

I lay on my stomach with my head in my arms to try to calm down. Every time the water rippled I expected to see Solo's canoe glide around the corner, and my pulse would beat faster. But after lots and lots of repeated rippling, it slowly became clear that Solo wasn't showing up. The sun had dipped well below the trees, which meant it had to be close to dinnertime.

Part of me was immensely relieved, but another part felt ashamed. I knew exactly why he hadn't come. I was nothing like him or any of his friends. Or my father. I didn't fit in anywhere.

I pulled Mr. Little from my pocket and studied his frozen face. It seemed the only place I belonged was in my imaginary world, one that would never exist.

As I stood and wandered back to the house to see if dinner was ready, my whole body felt sore from stacking wood, but there was a deeper ache somewhere in my chest that got worse the more I thought about Solo.

"There you are," said Tess. A large pot was steaming on top of the stove. "Wash your hands and go ahead to the dining room for July Dinner."

"What's July Dinner?"

"First Saturday of the month, the family's required to eat together in the dining room."

"Why?"

"I don't know why. It's just the way it's always been here. To celebrate the month ahead, I suppose. Ned's off the island, so it will be just the two of you."

"The two of who?"

"You and Lenore."

"What?! What about you?"

"I'm not part of the family, Martin. I *work* for the family."

The thought of eating alone with Aunt Lenore in that dusty dining room immediately ruined my appetite.

"But we're barely related! And she doesn't even recognize me most of the time!"

"Don't worry about it. She's in a good mood this evening," said Tess, shooing me away. "Now go on."

Aunt Lenore sat at the head of the table wearing yet another weird old dress. This one had pale purple ruffles strangling her neck.

"Aren't you the summer guest who's come to paint the house?" she croaked.

I nodded cautiously from the doorway, deciding it was best to agree with whatever she said. She pointed at a shelf as I entered the room.

"Well, you might as well take a place setting and have a seat."

I reluctantly picked up silverware, then turned and examined the long table. I didn't want to sit at the opposite end, directly across from her, so I chose the chair farthest to her left, where the bird had been standing the day before. I avoided looking directly at her, staring down at my lap instead like I was praying to survive the meal.

"*Ding-dong!*" she cawed and rang a small bell next to her fork. "We're famished!"

"Coming," replied Tess, bursting through the door carrying two plates of food. "I hope you like trout chowder, Martin," she said as she placed one of the plates in front of me. It held a bowl of chunky white soup, a roll, and two slices of tomato. This was a celebration?

"Where's the clotted cream?" Aunt Lenore demanded.

Tess handed her a tiny pot with a small knife and said, "I'll be right back with ice water."

The old lady lifted the tiny pot with her wobbly, spotty, wrinkly claw and stretched her arm toward me. "Clotted cream?"

Whatever that was sounded awful. I shook my head.

"Can't you speak?" she squawked.

I nodded.

"Well then, say something! If I have to share the table with another human being, at the very least, I expect a conversation."

I racked my brain trying to think of something to talk about while she cut her roll in half and greased it with heaps of that clotted goop. Then I remembered.

"How was your party?"

She glared at me suspiciously from the corners of her eyes. "What party?"

"Um, your garden party?"

At that moment Tess returned with a pitcher of water and filled Aunt Lenore's glass. After taking a long sip, she turned to Tess.

"What is that boy talking about? He asked me about a garden party."

"He must be confused," Tess replied, suddenly frowning at me. "Will you have your tea now, or later in front of the fire?"

"Later," said Aunt Lenore as she dipped her roll into her soup and took a large, sloppy bite.

"But it was yesterday morning?" I persisted. "You helped her with—"

Tess cut me off. "Ring the bell if you need me, you two. I'll be in the kitchen."

I couldn't understand why it was so wrong to ask about a party. What was I allowed to talk about?

As soon as Tess was gone, Aunt Lenore leaned across the table and squinted. "You're Samuel's friend, aren't you?"

I was startled by this question, but I nodded.

"Thought so. I've seen you boys down at the dock."

I couldn't help blurting, "You have?"

Everyone seemed to be watching everyone else on this island, as if they were all spying on each other.

She nodded. "And by the way," she whispered, "there was no garden party."

Wait, she did remember talking about it? What was I supposed to say now?

"Um . . . yeah. I kind of noticed that you didn't have any guests."

Aunt Lenore grinned. It was the first time I'd seen her smile, and it changed her whole face. She almost looked . . . nice.

"Good. I like it when young people are observant."

It felt weird to be complimented for saying something obvious. "Then you must not know many young people," I said before I realized I was saying it.

She raised her eyebrows. "Oh? You don't think you're observant?"

"I—I don't know." I shrugged. "I mean, it doesn't take a genius to see that people don't really come to this house for parties. Or for anything."

For a second I panicked, wondering if I sounded rude. But she just chuckled.

"I guess I've scared everyone off, more or less."

"Good guess," I blurted again, then stuffed a piece of bread in my mouth to keep quiet.

"Are *you* scared of me, young man?"

"Um . . ." I couldn't say yes, could I? But I had a feeling Aunt Lenore would know if I was lying. I finished chewing and swallowed hard. "It kind of depends?"

"Hmm." She nodded as if this was a very reasonable answer. All at once she seemed a lot more normal. Except not normal at all. Better than normal, if that was possible. Maybe this was what she was like before she started losing her memory. In a way I felt like I was meeting her for the first time.

"So, my name is Martin Hart," I said. "I don't

know if you remember meeting me a few—"

"Of course I remember you!" she interrupted, then leaned toward me across the table. In a hushed voice, she continued, "Someday, when you grow old and feeble, Martin, and every bone in your body aches, remember this golden nugget. People will do and say all kinds of things around you if they think you're bonkers."

My mouth dropped open. She was faking her memory loss? On purpose?

She leaned in even closer and pointed at my face.

"It's true. Take your father, for instance. He's planning to pull one over on me, isn't he? He wants to inherit this island when I'm dead, and he thinks I'm senile enough to leave it to him in my will."

"What? No. He . . ." Then I trailed off. Dad *had* said he wanted to inherit the island. And he hadn't been too surprised that Aunt Lenore seemed to be losing her memory—even though he hadn't said anything to me about that beforehand. "He said he just wants to make you happy," I stammered.

Aunt Lenore snorted. "If he had my happiness in mind, he wouldn't have dropped you off here with so little warning, and without asking for permission."

"He said you *invited* me . . ."

"Invited you? Why would I do that? I haven't heard a word from your father for, well, it must be at least fifteen years. In fact, the last time I saw him, I told him not to bother coming back again unless he drastically adjusted his worldview."

"His what?" As soon as I said it, I felt stupid. I knew what a worldview was, at least I thought I did. Embarrassed, I slipped a whole tomato slice in my mouth.

"It's the way Jonathan treats people. The way he *thinks of* certain people. Oh, I gave him quite a talking-to. Sent him off with his tail between his legs."

My mouth dropped open again, and this time the tomato slice almost fell out. I was so confused. Dad had said they were close! He hadn't said anything about Aunt Lenore chasing him away.

But it was true that he hadn't been here in ages.

"I think it's safe to say he hasn't changed a bit," Aunt Lenore went on. "He definitely wants this island for himself—probably so he can sell it for a pile of money and retire early."

"But—Dad loves this island," was all I could think to say. After all, he'd spent a gazillion years talking about how great this place was and how much he missed it . . .

"Is that what he told you? Well, I'm sure it's what he'd like everyone to believe. But he doesn't realize that I can see through him. Notice how he showed up here with you and tried to convince me the whole thing was *my* idea. Didn't even blink, did he? Believe me, he would've been a lot more careful if he knew I had my wits about me. It's a powerful weapon, the mind. Or lack of it."

At this point, I had no idea what to believe. I wasn't even sure Aunt Lenore actually had a clue what she was talking about. She might *say* her forgetfulness was just an act, but for all I knew, she really was losing her grip on reality.

Aunt Lenore raised her eyebrows and tilted her head, as if waiting for me to respond. Something about the way she looked at me convinced me that she was telling the truth. At least about her own sanity.

"You're not as scary as you seem," I said.

She smiled. "I'm glad you think so. Now raise your glass, Martin, and let's make a toast."

I lifted my water a few inches above the table.

"Here's to secrets between friends, imaginary gatherings, and of course, the Great and Beautiful Beyond."

What a weird toast. But I liked it. Though I

wondered if she knew her *Great and Beautiful Beyond* sign had broken a long time ago.

Aunt Lenore stretched her arm as far as it would go and clanked her cup against mine, spilling water from both of our glasses.

"Your turn," she said.

I was at a loss for words. Then I said the first thing that came to mind.

"Happy July?"

Aunt Lenore beamed as if I'd said something brilliant. "To July, the magical month when dreams come true!" she cried.

We clinked glasses again, this time meeting in the middle. Then I finally took a sip of the thick white gloppy chowder. To my surprise, it was delicious.

CHAPTER FIFTEEN

After dinner I escaped upstairs, closed my bedroom door, slipped off my sneakers, and climbed on top of the giant bed. Mr. Little rolled out of my pocket. I studied his miniature face.

"I don't know how we ended up in this crazy house," I said, "but I'm sure glad I brought you along."

What was going on around here? I definitely couldn't call these past few days boring. Every moment seemed to bring something unexpected. It was getting kind of overwhelming. I liked life to be orderly and predictable. On the other hand, I had never felt more like myself than I did here. No one acted like I wasn't normal. I could be whoever I wanted to be.

The seam on the edge of Mr. Little's leg had come loose. I propped him against the lamp on the nightstand, where he spent nights guarding me.

"It's probably not a good idea to carry you around anymore while we're stuck here," I explained. "I don't want to lose you again. Or have you fall apart."

Usually, I could tell what he was thinking just from his expression. But tonight his face was flat and blank. So I slid the drawer open and tucked him inside.

Just then something struck the side of the house. I got off the bed and looked out the window, but it was dark now, especially here in the woods. A stick bounced off the glass right in front of my face. Startled, I jumped back. Then I slowly opened the window and peered down at the ground. It was Solo.

"I'm coming up," he whispered loudly. "Tie this to the bed."

"Tie what?"

Next thing I knew a clump of rope hit me in the chest, then fell back to the ground.

"Concentrate, Martian," he said in a louder voice, gathering up the rope. "Try again."

This time I caught it.

"Got it!"

"Shhhhhhh," he warned me. "Keep it down."

"Now what do I do with it?"

"Pretend the bed post is the pole on a dock and you're tying off a boat."

"Um, doing what to a boat?"

Solo said nothing for a second, then replied, "Just drop it down."

Next thing I knew he threw the rope back at me, but this time one end was tied in a circle.

"Loop it over the bed post," he whispered loudly.

I did what he said, then flung the other end out the window. Within a minute, Solo scurried up the side of the house in his bare feet like a mountain climber.

"How did you do that?"

He slipped over the window ledge into my bedroom. "It's easy with a good rope. I hid it behind the house this morning so I could climb up when I needed to."

"When you needed to what?"

"To find you."

My throat got that tight feeling again and my heart sped up so fast I had to take a breath.

"You aren't mad at me?"

"Why would I be mad at you?"

"Because I can't, you know, do anything."

"I don't know what you're babbling about, Martian, but we need to get out of here."

"Now?"

"Everyone's already at the campground and the bonfire's huge. I need to get back."

"But—but—but I thought you said when the sun is just above the trees? And and it's dark now, and what if Tess—"

"We'll be back before it gets too late. No one will notice." I watched as he retied the rope around the bedpost using complicated knots. "That should hold both of us. Now follow me down," he said as he dipped his head through the open window and disappeared.

Follow me down?

I leaned outside and saw the top of Solo's head as he dropped quickly to the ground and looked up.

"Piece of cake, Martian, I'm right here!"

Something about the way he said that made me trust him. And I realized I had never truly trusted anyone before, and that maybe if Solo believed I could do this, it meant I really could.

So I took deep breaths as I tied my sneakers tight and forced myself to focus, the same way I do just before I enter the last obstacle in an incredibly challenging video game. As I held the rope, I pulled my left leg through the window and, suddenly, I was airborne. I'm not sure if my shoes ever touched the side of the house, but my hands burned by the time my feet slammed into the ground.

"I did it!"

Solo grinned. "Good enough," he said and then lowered his voice like we were on a secret mission. "Follow me and stay low till we're past the kitchen window."

We could hear the sink running and Tess doing the dishes as we crawled along the bottom of the house. Once on the trail and in the woods, we stood up again. Solo ran swiftly, like a cat, down to the dock in the darkness, while I struggled to keep up with him.

"Get in," he said as he untied the canoe.

I sat on the edge and dangled my feet. The boat looked extremely unstable. I didn't know how to get in. What if I fell in the water and drowned?

As if reading my mind, Solo got down on his knees and pulled something out of the boat. It was an orange life jacket.

"Here. It's big, but it'll work until you learn how to swim."

I didn't know what to say. The fact that he'd thought to bring it and the way he gave it to me, as if it were completely normal to not be able to swim, made me like him even more. I pulled it over my head and pulled the straps as tight as I could. It almost came down to my knees, but it was perfect.

"We need to hurry," he said holding the boat's pointy front end. "Put your feet on the bottom and get in sideways."

I took another deep breath and slid butt-first onto the middle seat, feeling a bit better now that I had a life jacket and knew I wouldn't drown. Solo slipped in behind me and pushed us away from the dock with a swift flick of his paddle.

Soon we were moving, but I had no idea where, since I immediately gripped the sides of the boat and squeezed my eyes shut. I did my best to ignore the swoosh of the water and the scary thoughts about the deep dark mucky bottom and the creatures that lived below.

After a few minutes of paddling, Solo said quietly, "Full moon."

I tilted my head back and opened one eye. The sky was massive, bigger and clearer than any sky I had ever seen. The sun had set behind the distant navy blue mountains, leaving faint purple lines across the horizon. Stars flickered faintly, and off to the right in the darkest part of the sky, a perfectly round moon glowed. I wondered how it could be the same moon I had seen all my life in Delaware. I'd never thought about all the other faraway places the moon watched over every night.

I took a long breath and rolled my head forward and gazed out over the lake. It was black and still, except for the pattern our canoe made slicing through the water. Miles of dark liquid extended in front of us.

"Prophet's Beach is up there around that bend," said Solo, and my stomach clenched again. All those wild boys would burst our perfect bubble. I finally felt safe out here and, more than anything, wanted to stay on the quiet water alone with Solo and drift for hours.

As we followed the curve of the lake, the faint smell of smoke filled the air. Soon I could make out a break in the trees: a beach area. Solo paddled the canoe onto the mainland and I got out first, surprised at how shaky my legs felt. The shore was a thin ribbon of rocks and sand, and in the distance, up an incline, a campfire glowed. Solo stepped into the water in his bare feet and shoved the boat higher onto the beach to make sure it wouldn't float away. Then he ran off through the tall weeds toward the flames on the hill.

"Come on!" he shouted without looking back.

I had no choice. If I stayed here, everyone would wonder why Solo had brought a kid to the roast who refused to leave the beach. I dropped my life jacket in the boat, forced my feet to march forward, and tried to think about something else, anything else. I wouldn't think about the fact that the sky was getting even darker by the second, or that strange animal noises were growing louder, or that now something was flying near . . . *my head.*

All at once, little birds were swarming me like in a horror movie.

"*Ahhhhhh!*" I screamed and tore up the path as fast as I could toward the fire pit, waving my arms to shoo the creatures away.

I stopped short in front of the bright blaze, still swiping at the air.

"A bunch of crazy birds tried to attack me!" I yelled.

Solo burst into laughter.

"They're bats, Martian. They won't bother you—look up."

Directly above us, dozens of tiny winged

shadows darted back and forth across the night sky. I ducked automatically.

"They want moths and mosquitoes," he explained, "not you."

Suddenly remembering that other boys must have just seen my performance, I squinted past the flames and scanned the area. But no one else was there.

"Where is everybody?"

He picked up a stick with a pinecone on the end and held it over the fire.

"I guess we're too late—we missed them. I thought at least Clam would still be around and you could meet each other."

The pinecone lit up and crackled like a huge match. Solo swirled it, making designs in the black air. A wave of relief washed over my body, but at the same time, I felt guilty for messing up his evening. After all, it was my fault he had to come all the way into my bedroom to get me.

Just then, a loud terrible screech came from the woods.

"What was that?"

"It's just a fisher—a kind of giant weasel that makes a lot of noise. Geez, relax, Martian. I won't let anything eat you."

It hadn't occurred to me that anything would want to eat me, but I felt a little better knowing that Solo would protect me. So I tried to relax, like he said, and not think about the giant screeching weasel. I sat down on the ground near the fire.

Solo handed me a branch with a clump of pine needles. "Wanna roast it?"

I took the branch and held it far enough from the flame so it wouldn't actually burn. Fire made me nervous. But I liked the way this one smelled, like a hundred Christmas trees.

Off in the distance a flash of light caught my eye. It was blinking near the top of one of the dark mountains. At first I assumed the flames were playing tricks on my eyes, but the light kept beaming from the same spot.

"Hey, look way up there." I pointed. "Do you see that?"

"Yep," he mumbled, but he hardly glanced.

The light seemed to be blinking in a pattern, like a code. It reminded me of something I'd seen in an old war movie my dad had made me watch—people sending messages with lights.

"Are there people up there? Is that a special signal? Do you think they're okay?"

"Probably just someone out taking a walk with a flashlight," he replied.

"At night?" I asked. "On the top of a mountain?"

But he didn't respond.

"I really think they're trying to say something," I said, but Solo remained uninterested.

After another minute the light disappeared. I turned back and stared at the fire, which was now barely burning. Solo held his chin in one hand and continued poking at the small flames with his charred branch.

Without knowing why, I changed my mind and lit the pine needles at the end of my stick. They crackled and popped like mini fireworks. We both watched but said nothing until the sparking stopped and I threw the branch into the red coals. Solo stood and smiled down at me as if I had passed some secret test.

"We should head back now, Martian."

CHAPTER SIXTEEN

As we moved across the lake, I had no choice about keeping my eyes open. Solo said I had to look out for rocks since it was so dark. A million-trillion stars twinkled against the black velvet sky. And the moon glowed just enough for us to follow the shoreline back to Beyond.

"Where do you live exactly?" I whispered. The darkness made it easier to ask "loaded" questions.

"Up that way," he said, but I couldn't really see where he was pointing.

"Do you have any brothers or sisters?"

He answered quietly, "Not that I know of."

It was obvious he didn't want to talk about his family, so I talked about mine.

"I don't either. I always wished I did. But my parents had me when they were already pretty old, so they didn't want to chance it."

Solo stopped paddling and asked, "Chance what?"

The boat silently drifted. It occurred to me I had never thought about what my parents meant when they gave me that answer.

"I'm not sure. I think older parents are more likely to have babies with health problems . . . or something like that."

As we approached the island, the full moon dimly lit the dock as if it were the setting for a play. I had been in some school productions when I was younger, just small parts, but the sets were what really interested me. Creating perfect, pretend worlds out of nothing.

Solo told me to grab the ladder to pull myself up. Getting out of the canoe was much easier than getting in.

"Thanks for the life preserver," I said as I stood above him and unhitched the plastic buckles.

"Keep it, at least while you're here."

"Are you sure?"

He dipped the paddle into the water and moved noiselessly backward.

"See ya tomorrow, Martian."

"Really?" I called. "You'll be back tomorrow?"

"Why wouldn't I?"

I watched as he disappeared into the shadows.

Even though we had practically just met, I got such a strong feeling every time Solo left. But tonight it felt worse. It was hard to describe, kind of like a homesick feeling. Like I'd never see him again . . . and I wanted to see him all the time.

Standing in the dark, listening to the water slap against the dock, I stared up at the sparkles blanketing the sky. I had never been outside alone at night, mostly because the idea of getting lost in the dark had always terrified me. But now I couldn't believe how much I could see—and how much I could hear. Night sounds were very different from day sounds. Half of me still worried about the bats and the giant weasels and everything that might want to eat me. But the other half of me sort of liked it.

I managed to find the path hidden beneath the shadows, and I quickly followed the rocky trail up the small hill toward the house. I had no idea what time it was, or whether anyone at the house would still be awake, but I knew I couldn't climb up the outside wall using Solo's rope.

Luckily, the kitchen was empty when I sneaked in the back door, and except for a single lamp in the den by the fireplace, the house was dark. My footsteps creaked as I climbed the stairs carefully, trying not to wake Tess or Aunt Lenore. I tiptoed around the corner and switched on the light in my bedroom.

Standing in the middle of the room was Solo, holding the rope in his hands!

I almost screamed but managed to hold it in. "You scared me!" I said and shoved him.

He laughed hard and shoved me back.

"That look on your face was worth it," he said.

"Shhh!" I reached over and covered his mouth.

I was so happy to see him again. He backed away from my hand and quietly shut the door. Then he scanned the room.

"So what do you want to do, Martian?"

"Do?" I said. "Isn't it time to go to sleep?"

"You can sleep anytime," he said as he walked over to the corner bookcase. He took a book off the shelf, looked at its cover, and put it back. He did the same thing with all the other books. Then he got to the one on the end with the old newspaper clipping in it, the one I'd found my first day here. He pulled out the tattered article and stared at it for a second. I looked over his shoulder at the picture of the guy with the mustache who'd been arrested so many years ago.

"Pretty crazy, huh?" I said. Seeing it again made me wonder—why had someone saved that one newspaper article? And how had it ended up in this room folded inside an old book?

Solo didn't answer. He just slid the article back into the book and stuck it on the shelf. Then he grabbed an old thin paperback from the bureau. He pointed at the title above a picture of three heads floating around the sun. "What's this say?"

I leaned over to get a better look. "*The One That Got Away*."

He continued to stare at the cover, squinting a little.

"Do you need glasses?" I asked.

"I don't know," he replied. "I don't think so."

"Well, can you see the letters?"

He outlined them with the tip of his finger. "T, H, E," he said and spelled out each word. "Is it good?" he asked.

"Doubt it. It's so old, and it looks weird, and the

title doesn't make much sense. But I'm sure you can borrow it if you want."

"No point," he said.

"Why not? Tess wouldn't mind."

Then he mumbled something I couldn't hear.

"You can't *what?*" I asked.

"I. Can't. Read."

I had never met anyone who couldn't read. "Didn't they teach you how to read at school?"

"I don't go to school, not anymore. And when I did I just couldn't figure it out and none of the teachers seemed to care."

I didn't know which was stranger—that he couldn't read or that he didn't go to school.

He turned the pages gently as if they might break. Then he paused and stared at one of the crinkly yellow pictures. All at once I had the perfect idea, something that both of us could do together.

"I can read it to you if you want."

I couldn't believe I'd just said that, because I was a terrible read-aloud reader when the teacher called on me in class. I had no problem reading to myself, but when I had to read out loud in front of others, my tongue got thick and I could barely get a sentence out of my mouth.

Solo's whole face smiled. He brushed the dirt off his bare feet with his hand and jumped up on my enormous bed.

"Start at the beginning, Martian," he beamed. "I want to hear the whole story."

CHAPTER SEVENTEEN

The next morning I woke with a start, still dressed in yesterday's clothes and huddled under the quilt. I remembered reading the tattered little book to Solo the night before and then at some point turning off the light because he had fallen asleep next to me. But now there was no sign of him.

I sat up and looked around the room. The rope was at the far end of the bed, and the windows were closed. I fell back against the pillows and tried to remember what had happened, to make certain I hadn't dreamed it.

That little book had been impossible to understand, some kind of mystery written in the fancy way people used to talk. But Solo listened closely, and when I asked him if he actually liked it, he said, "I like any book," which I thought was a strange thing for him to say since he couldn't read.

He'd curled up on his left side and watched me the entire time, his hands wedged under his head instead of the pillow. I had never read so much in my life, especially something that made almost no sense, but I didn't care. I was finally able to do something for Solo, the one thing he couldn't do for himself.

Once we'd gotten about a quarter of the way through the book, I turned to ask him if I should keep going, but he had fallen asleep. I held my fingers close to his mouth and could feel a tiny stream of warm air. I leaned back, turned off the lamp, and fell asleep next to him, his breath blowing against my face. It was the first time I felt truly happy to be on the island.

Now, anxious to go and find Solo, I put on my sneakers without bothering to change the clothes I had slept in, something I never would have done just a week ago.

The stairs creaked extra loudly as I sneaked down the stairs hoping to slip through the house undetected.

"You got in late last night."

Aunt Lenore's voice came from the other side of the rocking chair, which was pushed up right in front of the low crackling fire. I couldn't believe she knew I had been out. Did Tess know too?

Aunt Lenore bent her arm and motioned me closer with one of her long bony fingers. I was sure I was in trouble. I took a deep breath and stepped toward her. A thick pile of blankets was pulled up to her chin. She swiveled her head.

"Did you boys have a nice time?"

I wasn't sure if this was a trick question, but I nodded anyway. Obviously, it was impossible to hide anything around here.

"Good," she whispered and smiled. Then she closed her eyes and rested her head back against the chair as the blankets slipped away from her chin.

Good? That was it?

"Aunt Lenore?"

"Mm?"

"How do you know Samuel?"

"Oh, I've known pieces of that family all my life."

"You have? What're they like?"

She grunted, her eyes still closed. "Just like him—stubborn, proud, intent on taking care of themselves. My kind of people. But they've mostly scattered now. There's just Samuel and Isaac, and a few of Isaac's dubious kin, in the area . . ."

"Who's Isaac?"

"His great-grandfather."

I was surprised Solo hadn't mentioned him. And why did that name sound so familiar?

"Does he live with him?"

"Sometimes. Mostly in the cold months. But I've seen that child running around out here even in the dead of winter . . . Ah, the vitality of youth."

Her voice was starting to fade and I could tell she was about to fall asleep, but I still had so many questions. "What about his parents? Where are they?"

"Goodness knows," sighed Aunt Lenore. "The father was always an unknown quantity. And his mother hasn't been heard from in years."

I guess I'd known there were kids in the world who didn't have parents, but I'd always assumed those kids still had someone to take care of them. I couldn't imagine being all alone. Maybe Solo wasn't as happy as he seemed.

Aunt Lenore's head and shoulders had settled farther into the chair, and her breathing had grown slow and even. I crept carefully out of the room, so I wouldn't wake her, and then rushed down the long hall to the kitchen.

"Look at you, up already!" said Tess. "Though

you did go to bed quite early. Are you feeling fully recovered from your bout with the berries?"

I was relieved Tess didn't know what Aunt Lenore had somehow figured out.

"I'm feeling great!" I said as I edged toward the back door. "But I need to look for something I think I lost by the dock yesterday."

"Oh no, not until you've eaten," she said as she spooned oatmeal into a bowl and placed it on the table. "You need to put some meat on those bones."

I sat down and devoured the oatmeal without bothering to add syrup. Tess sat next to me and watched, which made me nervous.

"About last night," she said, and I panicked and coughed on a mouthful of mush.

"Which part of last night?"

"Listen, don't worry about it. It was my fault."

I stared at my bowl, hoping to hide my guilty expression, although I wasn't sure which event of the night was making me feel most guilty.

"How could it be your fault?"

Tess leaned over and whispered next to my face.

"I should have explained to you about her *episodes*. But I didn't want to frighten you."

"Huh?"

She glanced in both directions and lowered her voice even more.

"It started a couple months ago. Lenore would announce she had plans to go to this or that, like the garden party. So I humored her and went along with it. After all, it occupied her time and gave her day a sense of dignity and purpose." Tess turned and checked the room before continuing. "But within a few minutes she would forget she ever insisted on it. And that would be that. All dressed up and no place to go."

She was talking about July Dinner . . . I exhaled and began eating again.

"So I guess what I'm saying is," she said in a more cheerful voice, "it's best to speak simply to your great-aunt, and always in the present tense. Talk about the weather, for example."

I couldn't help smiling to myself, thinking of last night's conversation with Aunt Lenore. It had had nothing to do with the weather. But then I remembered what she'd said about Dad. All at once I didn't feel like smiling.

"Got it," I said, and Tess patted my hand.

"Um, Tess? Whose idea was it for me to come visit this summer? I thought Aunt Lenore invited me. I mean, I thought she called my dad and asked him to bring me."

"Lenore, pick up a telephone?" Tess laughed. "No. I called your father about a month ago to tell him about Lenore's current state of mind. Since he's her closest family aside from Ned, I thought he should know. And then he called back a couple weeks later and told me he was thinking of bringing you out here. I said I'd have to ask Lenore about it, and when she woke up from her nap that day I did. She gave it some thought, then said, 'Yes, why not?' But she probably doesn't remember that now."

I scraped the empty bottom of the bowl with my spoon. So Dad *had* lied to me. He'd talked to Tess, not Aunt Lenore. And if he'd lied about that . . .

"Yeah, probably not," I mumbled.

As soon as I stepped outside into the fresh air I could hear the same hammering sound I had heard the previous morning. It seemed to be coming from the other side of the island. I walked down to the dock, and as I followed the shoreline the pounding grew louder until I was practically on top of the noise. And then, just like before, it suddenly stopped.

I climbed through the thick brush, past scratchy twigs, between huge boulders, and down a hill, trying to find the source. Ahead of me I saw a dip in the ground, with a tiny log cabin sitting in it, as if the earth were trying to swallow it. A crooked metal chimney stuck out of the metal roof, which was covered in large patches of moss. The front porch was just wide enough to hold a hammock at one end and a red rocking chair at the other.

I tiptoed to the side of the house and peeked through the window. A table and two chairs took up the center of the room, and I could see an old sink, a stove, and a small refrigerator lining the wall. It was shadowy, so I couldn't make out many details. "Just in time for a mug of joe!"

I spun around. Uncle Ned marched down into the dip carrying a backpack over his left shoulder. The white stubble I'd seen all over his face last time we met was now a beard.

For some reason, I felt ashamed, like I had been caught stealing something, even though I was just peeking in. "Someone's been hammering," I stammered, "and I was trying to figure out where it was coming from."

"Hmm . . . " he said and paused to listen. "Don't hear it."

He shook his backpack down his arm and placed it on the ground. His bones cracked as he stretched in different directions.

"Are you just getting back from your trip?" I asked.

The old man rolled his head around his neck and sighed. "Wasn't a trip exactly, but I was away."

Then he pulled a bottle from the back of his overalls and took a huge gulp.

"Cider?"

I shook my head. "No thanks."

"Well," he said, wiping his rough white beard with his other hand, "now that you're here, you might as well come on in."

CHAPTER EIGHTEEN

As soon as Uncle Ned turned on the lights, the tiny cabin came alive. The main part, a large colorful room, was split into two sections. The front room had a square red couch, a couple cozy chairs, and a wood stove. The other half was the yellow kitchen with two doors at the back wall, probably leading to his bedroom and a bathroom. It was very tidy but packed with stuff, like old photographs and chunks of twisted wood and harmonicas and jigsaw puzzles and tons more. His house felt kind of like a museum, but an interesting museum. I wanted to look at every single thing.

The best parts were the easels he had in almost every corner with brushes and jars of bright paint stacked on tables and stools nearby. Artwork hung on the walls wherever there was space.

"Are you an artist?" I asked.

He filled a metal coffeepot with water and placed it on the small stove. It took him a few tries for the gas flame to light. "Some might say that."

There was a tapping on the front door.

"Oh, that'll be Poe," he said. "He must know I'm back."

Uncle Ned took a handful of seeds from a jar, grabbed an apple from the refrigerator, and opened the door. That same black bird from Aunt Lenore's house was now standing on the porch as if waiting for someone to come out and play. He cocked his head back and forth until Uncle Ned threw the seed and apple over the steps and into the bushes.

"There's your breakfast," he called out as the bird hopped toward the food. Then he said to me, "I try not to give him meat so he'll still hunt for that, although he's getting lazy."

"Does he always tap on the door?" I asked.

"Only when he's hungry," he replied, as if the bird were a person.

"I saw him a couple days ago," I said, "eating something off the dining room table."

Uncle Ned laughed and walked back to the

kitchen area. "Lenore loves the little guy, but poor Tess can't stand having anything *wild* in the house unless she can cook it."

He placed two mugs on the table, plus a plate of soft butter, knives, spoons, and a small bowl full of biscuits. I moved closer to a painting on an easel leaning against the couch, a picture of a cottage built into the side of a hill. Goats were grazing in the steep front yard under a blue sky filled with twinkling flashes of light.

"Do you like sugar and milk in your coffee?"

I turned. "You mean me?"

"Well, I'm not asking Poe, too hot for him."

I had never tried coffee and was pretty sure I wasn't allowed to drink it. "I guess so," I said and sat down at the small table. "Thanks."

The biscuits were delicious, but I had to add a lot of milk and sugar to the coffee to make it drinkable. Uncle Ned chewed a long time after each bite, like he was chewing a big piece of steak. Crumbs stuck to his beard.

I remembered Solo had said he'd met Ned. I wondered if they also sat together at this table and drank coffee.

"Do you know Solo—I mean, Samuel?"

He poured more coffee into his mug. "Want some more?"

"No thanks."

He added a heaping spoonful of sugar. "Yep, I know him."

"Tess says he's a wild child."

Uncle Ned nodded and grinned, like that was a good thing to say about someone. "Samuel knows how to take care of himself. He always has."

"How come he doesn't have to go to school?"

"Well, for one thing there isn't one around here anymore. I forget where the closest one is—at least an hour away. "

"But isn't it, like, the law that kids have to go to school?"

"I guess you could say that Samuel comes from a family that's never been too keen on the law. Honestly, I'm not much of a fan of school myself. Kids like Samuel, sometimes it does 'em more harm than good, I think. Crushes their spirit. Doesn't teach them much except that they're different and that according to the people in charge they're always going to fail."

I wasn't sure I was following him, but that last sentence felt familiar—like it was something I'd always been thinking, in the back of my mind, about myself.

Just then, a clap of thunder interrupted our conversation. I realized it had gotten dark outside. Uncle Ned pushed his chair back, threw open the front door, and hurried out onto the porch.

"Here it comes!" he called back through the open door. Rain poured down in sheets, pounding the metal roof overhead so hard it sounded like rocks. Wind blew through the cabin, causing everything to flutter at the same time. Uncle Ned closed the door quickly and returned to the table.

"You might as well stay until the storm is over," he said, picking up another biscuit. "Do you like to paint?"

The only paintings I had ever done were finger paintings in art class when I was in elementary school. The middle school art teacher, Ms. Tan, preferred crafty projects like making baskets out of used pizza boxes. But Uncle Ned gave me the easel by the couch, replacing the cottage-and-goat painting with a fresh piece of thick white paper.

"Here's a set of watercolors," he said as he placed a tray of paints and a small bowl of water on a stool next to the easel. Then he gave me one of his old button-down shirts to use as a smock. I had to roll up the sleeves to make it fit.

"What should I paint?"

Uncle Ned glanced around. "How about the rain?"

I thought about that for a second. "How do you paint rain?"

"However you want to paint it."

So for the next hour, I brushed strokes of gray and black and pale blue behind a window framed in red polka-dot curtains. I liked how the bowl of water changed color each time I rinsed a brush.

Uncle Ned dabbled around the cabin, rearranging things in cabinets and sweeping the floor, while the rain fell outside. Once in a while he would stand behind me and make a comment like "Nice" and "You have a good eye." His voice was very low and reassuring.

"Finished!" I finally announced and stepped back to take a better look.

"Be right there," Uncle Ned called from the kitchen, where he was washing clothes in a plastic tub. As he peered around the corner, drying his hands with a dish towel, his eyes grew big with surprise.

"Well," he said. "Isn't that something?"

"Do you wanna keep it?"

He folded the dishtowel and smiled. "I'd like that very much," he replied and studied the walls. "I'll hang it right over there above the sofa so I can see it from every angle."

I thought about my father's reaction when Tess told him that Uncle Ned still lived on the island, as if that were a bad thing. I wondered why. Ned was one of the nicest grown-ups I had ever met.

"Did my dad ever do this?" I asked.

"Do what?"

"Paint?"

He crossed his arms and wrinkled his bearded face, then shook his head. "Not that I'm aware."

"Aunt Lenore says he has a problem with his worldview."

Uncle Ned laughed. "That's the sort of thing my sister would say."

"I didn't really understand what she meant by that," I said, hoping to learn more.

"Well," he replied, smiling, "most likely she felt he did a lot of running around and not enough sitting still and paying attention to things. Not enough painting, in a way."

The rain had stopped, and now sunbeams streaked through the same window. Uncle Ned opened the front door. The air smelled new, like cut grass and flowers, and little birds chirped loudly, celebrating the end of the storm. Immediately I thought about Solo and wanted to find him and tell him about my visit.

"I'd better get going now," I said, "but thanks for the coffee and biscuits, and for letting me paint."

"Wait one more minute," said Uncle Ned as he disappeared into a room at the back of the kitchen. He returned holding a smooth round wooden box. Inside were beautiful sparkling rocks, like treasures in a treasure chest.

"This is mica," he explained, "quite common in these parts, but aren't they magical the way they glimmer just so?"

I picked up the largest piece, shiny silver with glowing streaks.

"Wow . . . I really like it."

"You can keep that one, Martin, as a reminder of your summer here."

I didn't know what to say. I didn't have anything this wonderful at home, but it was exactly the kind of interesting thing I liked to keep under my fuzzy green pillow. It was as if this old man knew me better than I knew myself.

CHAPTER NINETEEN

I thought if I hung around the usual places, Solo would magically appear like he always did. But he didn't show up the whole day. Not while I worked on Soloville (which needed some minor repairs after the rainstorm), or during lunch in the kitchen with Tess, or even later when I stacked more wood in the shed.

The sun was setting over the tops of the trees and the dock rocked in the wind as I sat on the edge gazing across the water. I imagined he was out with Clam and their gang of friends, jumping off cliffs or cooking over a bonfire. Hanging around me too much had to be boring for a wild child like Solo. *Unless,* I thought, *I could make myself more interesting or useful.*

That's when I remembered the tall shelves crammed with books in the den, so I headed back to the house to see if I could find a good one for us to read.

As usual, Aunt Lenore was dozing in the rocking chair by the fireplace, a teacup and half-eaten scone with jam on the table next to her. To my surprise, Poe stood perched on the windowsill, pecking the feathers under his wings. Scratchy opera music sang from an old-fashioned record player in a shadowy corner of the room. Like always, Aunt Lenore wore a long dress, this one faded white. I tiptoed past her.

"Looking for something?" Her owl eyes, now wide open, seemed to stare through me.

"Books?" I replied. "Something to read."

"Help yourself."

I knelt down to search through the bottom shelf. Every book was so worn I could barely read the letters printed on the hard spines. Most of the faded titles didn't make sense, with words like *Transcendentalism* and *Corvids*.

"Funny," she mumbled. "I don't recall Jonathan or Jason reading anything when they were here. Not even those ridiculous comic books."

The mention of my dad surprised me. "You remember them staying here?"

She leaned forward and scanned the room—checking to make sure Tess wasn't nearby, I figured. "Of course I remember," she whispered, and then settled back into the creaky chair. The white lace below her neck fluttered as she slowly breathed in and out.

I wanted to ask more questions, but something about her felt unpredictable, as if she could transform into someone else without warning. I turned back to the books and pulled one from the shelf. It was a manual on International Morse Code, exactly what I had been trying to remember when Solo and I saw the blinking light.

"This is between you and me," said Aunt Lenore. "Those two were a pain in the neck."

I twisted back. She was in the same position, her eyes still closed, as if she was talking in her sleep. Poe seemed to be dozing too.

"They were?"

"Oh, were they ever! Loud and raucous, splashing and hollering and disturbing the peace. And the worst table manners. I had a headache from the day they arrived until the day they left."

I couldn't help giggling. According to Dad, he had shared some special bond with Aunt Lenore when he was a kid. But now it turned out she'd never even liked him. I'd always assumed that everything he'd told me about his childhood was true. But maybe it was only his version of the truth, how he wanted to remember it. Did that mean he could be wrong about other stuff?

"And they had no respect for the island, as if the outdoors had been created solely for their benefit. Neither of them realized that quite the opposite was true."

I wasn't sure what she meant by that, but it reminded me of what she'd said about Dad's worldview—and his plan for Beyond. I still couldn't believe that Dad would just sell the island, after all the good times he'd had here. Unless he'd been lying about that the same way he'd lied about other things . . .

"You're different," she said, as she opened her eyes and studied me. "You're nothing like those two—or most boys, truth be told. You have—you know—*it.*"

Those words stabbed me like a knife. I couldn't believe Aunt Lenore, of all people, had just told me I wasn't normal. That I had something wrong with me. She'd been so nice for the past couple of days.

Why was she suddenly turning against me? All at once, I felt like crying.

"Like Samuel," she said. "There's another boy with plenty of *it*."

I blinked. "He has *it* too?"

She was rocking the chair back and forth, grinning, as if recalling a funny story. "Well, that's why you two get along so well. Birds of a feather flock together."

As soon as she said that, Poe bounced down from the windowsill.

"Oh, I don't mean you," she said to him. "You're a loner, like I am."

Just then the phone rang in the kitchen. The sound was so loud it vibrated through the floor. I jumped as if I'd gotten an electrical shock.

"Tess?" Aunt Lenore croaked loudly. "Telephone!"

"Excuse me, Aunt Lenore?" I grabbed the book and stood up shakily. "What do you mean exactly? What is *it*?"

"Oh you know, that certain je ne sais quoi."

"I don't know what that means either."

The phone continued to ring.

"*Tesssss?* Who on earth is bothering us now?"

"So is *it* a good thing or a bad thing?"

The ringing finally stopped.

"Heavens, it's a wonderful thing! It's a golden glow, a natural warmth and energy and honesty, a true curiosity about the world! It'll get you far in life. People told me I had it, just like you do, but alas it seems to fade with age . . ."

Slowly it dawned on me. Aunt Lenore *was* telling me I wasn't normal. But in a *good* way.

"Martin?" Tess appeared in the doorway. She glanced back and forth between me and Aunt Lenore, whose eyes were closed again as if she had been sleeping all along.

"Your mother is on the phone."

"Mom?"

"Oh, honey. How are you?"

It had been barely a week since I'd talked to my mother, but it seemed like a year had passed. So much had changed, and her voice felt very far away.

"I'm okay, but I'm glad you called. I—"

"Before you say anything, Martin, I want to apologize for forcing you to go to Maine."

The long cord stretched all the way to the back

door. Somehow, Poe had made it outside and I could see him through the screen. He was standing on a wooden bench, his head twitching back and forth as if he were listening to my conversation.

"You do?"

Then my mother spoke so quietly I could barely hear her. "As soon as your dad got back, I knew we had made a mistake. He seemed very upset about seeing the house so run down—and poor old Aunt Lenore, just a shadow of her former self. I've barely been able to . . ." Her voice drifted off so I couldn't hear that last part. "Anyway, my car's still in the shop but I finally got Dad to admit what a ridiculous idea this trip has been! I just wanted to let you know that we'll drive up tomorrow, if you can hang in there one more night."

I was speechless. What was happening? This was what I'd hoped for, but . . .

"Martin? Are you okay? Should we drive up right away?"

At that moment, Poe bounced down from the bench, spread his wings, and flew off.

"Actually, Mom, that's what I wanted to tell you. I don't want you and Dad to come at all. I want to stay."

CHAPTER TWENTY

That evening, I pretended to feel tired after a long day and asked Tess if I could eat dinner in my room. The truth was I hoped Solo would climb through my window again. I had so much to tell him and couldn't wait for us to read the book on International Morse Code together.

According to the author, you transmit a series of dots and dashes to represent letters. Like the letter A is a dot and a dash. It was invented a long time ago, in the eighteen hundreds, and back then people made a tapping sound using an electric telegraph system. But you can make the dots and dashes using almost any method, including flashes of light. So now I was positive the lights we saw flashing on top of the tall mountain had been Morse code.

I didn't want to get too far ahead in the book without Solo, so I closed it and pulled Mr. Little out of my night table. At first I thought I would tell him all about my day, starting with my painting at Uncle Ned's cabin and especially what Aunt Lenore had said about my golden glow. But it was funny—I didn't feel like talking to a little stuffed mouse. I examined his tiny face and tried to feel something, but whatever usually made him come alive was missing.

I slipped him back into the drawer without saying a word, next to the sparkling chunk of mica from Uncle Ned, and I pulled the rope from under the bed. It was still tied to the bottom of the post, waiting for Solo to climb up again. I opened the window wide and gazed through the trees. The sun had set behind the mountains, leaving trails of pink and orange streaks across the pale sky. Other than the usual outdoor noises, it was very quiet.

And then I heard something, a rustling below.

"Solo?" I whispered.

The sound paused for several seconds. Then I heard it again. A soft crackling through the trees.

"Is that you?" I said a little louder.

Another long silence, followed by a crunching

noise that quickly disappeared. I figured it had to be an animal, like a chipmunk . . . but there was something about the way it hesitated, as if it were listening to me.

I waited another minute, but whatever it was had gone. So I decided the best strategy was to climb into bed and go to sleep, since Solo seemed to appear only when I least expected him.

But he never showed up, and the next couple days were the same. No sign of him at all. I was beginning to worry he would never come back.

I visited Uncle Ned at his cabin again, and this time he taught me how to play backgammon. He also told me I had potential as an artist, that he could see it in my strokes. I had always liked art class at school, but no one had ever told me I was good. Come to think of it, no one had ever told me I was good at anything.

The next day, Tess showed me how to weed the vegetable garden after I finished stacking all the wood. She admired my neat rows, claiming the stacks of logs had never looked tidier, and said I had learned to spot a weed very quickly.

But nothing seemed to matter much without Solo.

At night, I kept busy by memorizing International Morse Code and practicing with my flashlight. A dot is a short blink. A dash is holding the light long enough to count three dots. Between the dashes and dots that make up one letter, you wait for a time that's equal to one dot. Between letters, you wait three dots. Between words, you wait the time it takes to count seven dots.

S = 3 dots
(wait 1 dot)
O = 3 dashes
(wait 1 dot)
L = dot, dash, 2 dots
(wait 1 dot)
O = 3 dashes

The weather got hot, hotter than I ever remembered it getting in Delaware. (Except everyone had air-conditioning back home, so I wasn't sure if that was true.) I had just finished lunch and wandered out onto the front porch, trying to think of some way to cool off, when I bumped into Aunt Lenore, who was reclined on a lounge chair. I was surprised to see her outside. Even in this heat, she still wore an old-fashioned dress with a long skirt, but at least this one had short sleeves. Her freckly, crinkled skin reminded me of old tissue paper left in a box.

"Why aren't you soaking in the lake?" she asked. Then she picked up a glass of lemonade filled with ice and took a long, slurpy sip.

I didn't dare confess to her that I didn't know how to swim. "I'm waiting for Solo—I mean Samuel," I said and sat down on the top step below *The Great and Beautiful Be* sign.

"Well, you aren't going to find him up here," she croaked as she flipped open a large crescent-shaped fan and slowly waved it in front of her face. "He'd be at the water on a horrid day like this. That's where *I* would've been in my younger, carefree days."

It was hard to imagine Aunt Lenore as anything but an old lady.

"Back when you had *it?*" I asked.

Her eyes softened and then her whole face seemed to melt. "Oh, yes. I was very adventurous back then, especially for a girl. A little too adventurous, some people would say. My fiancé certainly came to think so."

"You mean you used to be married?"

"Engaged. I didn't say anything about marriage.

In the end, it wasn't meant to be."

I didn't know what to say, so I mumbled, "Sorry."

"Oh, there's nothing at all to be sorry about. I was better off single. A lot of people in those days were after me for my money. Not that things are really so different now."

We sat in silence for a second. I tried not to think about her suspicions that Dad wanted to inherit the island just to sell it. So I found myself staring at her fan, which was covered in colorful birds. Strange lettering ran down the middle of each panel. I craned my neck to get a better look.

"I like your fan," I said. "What language is that?"

She turned it toward her chest and said, "That's a lovely and wise Chinese proverb."

"Do you know what it says?"

She hesitated before replying. "*A bird does not sing because it has an answer. It sings because it has a song.*"

I thought about that for several seconds, then asked, "Do you think people have songs too?"

She grinned. "I certainly hope so."

I looked back out at the lake, sparkling through the tall trees like it was inviting me to come for a swim. More than ever, I wished I knew how.

As if reading my mind, Aunt Lenore said, "Have

a look around for the yellow raft and go for a float. Ned keeps it in the woodshed somewhere."

Floating on a raft didn't sound like a bad idea, especially since I still had the life vest from Solo and I could stay close to shore where the water wasn't above my shoulders.

"Okay," I said to Aunt Lenore. "Thanks."

"But you didn't hear that from me," she added with a wink.

After changing into my swim trunks and clipping on the puffy orange vest, I charged into the woods and up the path toward the woodshed. Like always, I stopped to check on Soloville. To my surprise there was another new addition at the end of that mysterious road. A small building with a cross on the roof—was it a church? That didn't seem like something Solo would build.

I froze and peered around the woods, wondering if whoever did this was still in the area.

"Hello?"

If it wasn't Solo, could it be Uncle Ned? He was the only other person who could have possibly known about my secret village.

"Anyone there?"

I waited another minute, but nothing. The

mosquitoes were beginning to swarm me as sweat trickled down my ribs under the life vest, so I hurried on to the shed.

I found the yellow raft in a storage closet in the back. Luckily it was still mostly inflated, although covered in cobwebs. As soon as I got down to the water's edge, I rinsed it off. Gradually, I waded up to my ankles and past my knees as I held the raft with one hand and the dock with my other to steady myself. Soon the refreshingly cold water was up to my waist and the life preserver bobbed around my ears. I tried hard not to think about the muck and all the creatures lurking below and I lay down across the raft. With my right foot I pushed away from the dock and, before I knew it, I was drifting on top of the lake.

After a couple minutes it felt awkward resting on my stomach, the puffy orange vest pressing into my chest, so I carefully flipped myself over. But just as I raised my left leg to turn around, the raft folded— and I fell in.

Immediately I knew I was over my head, since nothing but freezing water rushed below my toes. At first I gasped and hollered, but then I remembered to let the life vest save me, the way my instructor had taught me to do in the pool. And as soon as I relaxed and counted my breaths, I was okay.

I moved my arms a little and kicked my feet, just like I was really swimming, and managed to grab the yellow raft gliding a few feet away. The deep water still felt cold but no longer frigid. I decided to take a chance and dip my head back as I held onto the raft with my right hand. Then I spread my arms out and lifted my legs.

"Hey! You're floating, Martian!"

As I whipped around, I sucked in a noseful of water and erupted into coughing and gagging. I kicked and thrashed and hacked until I felt a tug on the back of my life vest. Solo dragged me into shore. I stumbled out of the lake and collapsed onto my back. My nose and throat felt raw.

"That was the funniest thing I've ever seen," said Solo, as he lay down next to me and laughed. "One second your puffy orange body's silently floating and then all of a sudden you freak out like you saw a shark!"

I coughed a bunch and then burped. "You startled me."

Solo held his stomach as he laughed some more. "I sure did! Wish Clam could have seen that."

I waited until he stopped laughing.

"Is that where you've been?" I asked as I sat up and glared down at him. "With Clam and all your friends jumping off cliffs and having giant wrestling matches?"

Solo sat up, water dripping from his head and hair. He wore just a long pair of brown shorts that were too big for him. His wet cinnamon skin glistened in the sunlight.

"I've been everywhere and nowhere," he finally said with a shrug, offering no real explanation. "So, you wanna take that thing off and really learn how to swim?"

"I think I've gagged enough for one day," I said. "Besides, I wasn't trying to swim. I was just cooling off."

"Come on, you aren't pouting, Martian, are you?"

I *was* pouting, but it had nothing to do with making a fool out of myself just now. I was mad at Solo for deserting me for days, and envious of all those boys and that stupid Clam kid he obviously liked best of all. I wanted Solo to stay on the island with me and never leave.

We sat in awkward silence for a few minutes.

Then Solo stood up and threw a stone in the water. It landed way out in the middle of the lake.

"If you want to know the truth," he said as he threw another rock, "I've been working on something. Do you want to see it?"

CHAPTER TWENTY-ONE

I left my life vest on the dock to dry and followed him along the shore in the direction of Uncle Ned's cabin. But we passed right by the little log house and continued up the narrow path until we reached the opposite side of the island, where I'd never been. This side had a wide open view of the lake and of the mountains on the mainland. Solo stopped at the edge of the water and spun around, his green eyes wide with excitement.

"Don't you see it?"

I blocked the sun with my hand and scanned the water. "See what?"

He held my shoulders, twisted me around, and pointed up at the trees. A wooden structure stretched across two large branches. A tree house!

I had never seen a real homemade tree house, only the premade ones you could buy at stores. This one had lots of angles and was made out of old gray wood. A large hole had been cut into the wall facing the water.

"You built that?"

Instead of answering, Solo grabbed a rope ladder hanging beneath the tree and scrambled up. At the top, he pushed open a trapdoor and slipped in through the floor.

"Come on, Martian!"

I was amazed at how easy it was to climb the swinging rope ladder. Maybe I was already stronger than I'd been when I first got here. Once my head was inside, Solo took my arm and pulled me through, then closed the door behind us.

The little house was bare but, at the same time, cozy. There were five walls, no two the same size. A thick pile of rags and blankets covered one corner, and there was an old beach chair on the opposite side. A crate was used as a table in the center. Above the rectangular hole in the wall facing the lake, a wide sheet of black plastic was tied up with more rope. Solo saw me studying it.

"See? I even have a cover for the window in case it rains. And it keeps the bugs away at night."

"Do you sleep here?"

"Only in the summer. It used to be wide open, just a platform with railings. But I knew that would make you nervous, so I've been working on it the past few days, building walls. I wanted to do it before you left."

That same warm feeling rushed up my neck and across my cheeks.

"You built this for me?"

He shrugged like it was nothing. But what he didn't know was that no one, other than my mom, ever did anything for me or cared about what I might like. When I had asked Dad for a basic bicycle for my tenth birthday, he bought a mountain bike that was way too big for me, with twelve speeds and lightning bolts painted on the rims. Then he couldn't understand why I never rode it.

"All that hammering," I said, "that was you?"

"You could hear that on the other side of the island?"

"Just a little."

I poked around the space and noticed a cardboard box the size of a laundry basket tucked under one of the blankets. "What's in here?"

Solo opened it to show me. Inside I saw a wind-up music box, a dirty pink brush, a furry white jacket, and a framed photograph. I picked up the picture. It showed a teenage girl with long red hair. She stood in a field holding a very chubby baby. The picture was faded like it had been taken a long time ago.

"Who's this?"

At first, he didn't say anything. Then he murmured, "My mom. And that's me."

I laughed a little. "You were a fat baby."

He smiled, but he didn't laugh. I remembered what Aunt Lenore had said about his parents, and I immediately felt sad for him.

"Where's your mom now?" I asked.

Solo shrugged again like he didn't know what to say. I had a feeling that if he did say something, it would probably be about the fact that I asked too many questions.

Suddenly, he put the picture away and slid the box under the blankets. Then he turned to me and asked, "Do you want to sleep over tonight, Martian?"

Since the evening was still hot, Tess made a cold dinner of tomato sandwiches and pickles in the kitchen with the fans blowing. Then I announced I was extra tired from the heat, so I would read up in my bedroom for the rest of the evening. I felt a little guilty about not telling her the truth, but it wasn't like I was spending the night off the island.

Solo had told me to bring whatever I wanted, so I packed my pillow and soft pajamas in my backpack along with the book on International Morse Code (which I couldn't wait to show him) and my flashlight. On second thought, I removed my pajamas and packed an extra T-shirt instead. Then I washed my face, brushed my teeth, opened the window, and stared at the ground. I had two choices. I could slide down the rope, which was still stored under the bed, and leave now while it was light out—or I could wait another couple of hours until everyone was asleep, slip out the back door, and creep across the island in the dark.

I didn't have to think twice.

I swung the backpack over my shoulders, retied the rope to my bedpost and hung it out the window, and then climbed through and squeezed that rope as tight as I could until my feet slammed into the ground. It hurt a lot, but I couldn't help feeling proud. Only a week ago I had hesitantly ventured out of my bedroom for the first time to follow Solo down to the dock. Now I was sneaking through the shadowy woods to spend the night outside in his tree house!

Solo had told me to hoot like an owl twice when I arrived.

"Hoot-hoot!"

"Not bad, Martian."

He was sitting by the edge of the lake. His canoe was nearby, tucked under the bushes. He handed a paper bag to me.

"Want some?"

Inside were cookie pieces and lots of crumbs.

"Where did you get these?"

"Behind Only's. They put day-olds by the dumpster."

I examined the broken cookies crammed in the greasy bag. "What are day-olds?"

He looked confused. "Don't you have day-olds where you come from?"

I shrugged my shoulders exactly the same way Solo always did.

"It's food that doesn't sell the day it's made. They put a red sticker on it and mark it down. And when those still don't sell, they throw them out. That's when I get them. For free."

"You mean you get your food out of the garbage?"

"It's not *in* the garbage. It's on top."

For a second I couldn't think of anything to say. How was it possible that Solo's life could be so opposite from mine?

"Why don't you just ask Tess for something to eat?"

He took the bag from me and fished through it. "I don't want that food," he mumbled, "and I have plenty to eat."

Then he offered a chunk of cookie to a chipmunk who was venturing very close to our feet. Next thing I knew, the chipmunk ran up to Solo's fingers and grabbed the cookie with his front teeth.

"Wow!" I said.

Solo smiled. The chipmunk hid behind a tree to nibble on the morsel he held between his tiny paws.

"How did you get it to do that?"

"Simple. You train them by laying out a trail up to your fingers, and after a while they trust you enough to eat out of your hand. Wanna try?"

With my luck, the chipmunk would eat my thumb.

"Maybe another time."

Solo crumpled up the paper bag. "Did you bring your life vest?"

"No, why?"

He got up and shoved the canoe away from the bushes and into the water. "I want to show you where I hang out with my friends when it's really hot, like it was today."

Instantly, my stomach twisted into knots. I wasn't ready to meet his friends. I'd assumed it would be just the two of us all night.

"I better not go since I forgot the vest. I'll wait here for you."

Standing in water up to his knees, Solo held the canoe with his right hand. The hem at the bottom of his brown shorts was wet.

"What are you talking about? Get in, Martian. I'll keep the boat near the shore where it's shallow."

It looked like I had no choice. I removed my sneakers and socks, waded into the cold lake, and awkwardly climbed into the front seat. Solo handed me a paddle. I felt naked without the vest.

"This time you can help," he said.

"But I don't know what to do."

After settling in the back seat, he paddled in the air to demonstrate. "Dip into the water, pull it back, lift out, and circle. Don't worry about steering. That's my job."

It was actually easier than I thought it would

be, and it kept me from worrying about the gang of wild boys I was about to face. After a few frightening moments when we crossed the deep space between Beyond and the mainland, we stayed close to shore just as Solo had promised. A couple of times my paddle even bumped the bottom of the lake, so I wasn't worried about drowning anymore. But it looked like the sun was setting fast, so I really hoped this adventure wouldn't take too long.

"There it is," he said, pointing at a tall rock wall rising out of the water. "Pluto's Cliff."

I immediately remembered that this was the cliff he'd mentioned the first morning we met.

"What are we doing here?" I gasped.

"Relax," he replied. "We're not jumping. At least, not today."

I scanned the area for his wild friends, but I couldn't see any sign of other human life. We paddled to shore and slid the canoe beneath a small tree. Glancing straight up at the rock tower from directly below made me dizzy. Solo took off and scurried up the steep trail along the side of the cliff until he reached the top where the boulders were flat.

"It's easy!" he called down.

My legs felt so weak I thought I might have to sit

down. I reached into my pocket but then remembered I had left Mr. Little in the drawer in my bedroom. I looked up again. Solo leaned fearlessly over the ledge, as if he could stretch out his arms and fly.

"Do you want me to come down and help you?"

Something about the way he said that, as he bravely teetered close to the edge, gave me the confidence I needed to do it by myself. I dug the balls of my bare feet into the earth and climbed up that hill without looking back.

I got to the top a lot faster than I would've expected, sighed with relief, then took in the view of the lake. The mountains were turning bright blue as the sun set behind them.

Solo shoved my back lightly. "Don't fall!"

I panicked for a second, which made him laugh. Then he stepped in front of me, smiling inches from my face. I could tell he was as glad as I was that I'd actually made it.

"Where is everyone?" I asked.

He picked up his bare feet one at time to brush off the soles. "What do you mean?"

"All your friends you were talking about?"

"Oh, I don't know," he said. "They might stop by later."

I hoped not too much later. It was getting darker by the minute.

"So why is it called Pluto's Cliff?" I asked.

"It's just what people call it."

He pointed at an opening about the size of a beach ball, wedged between giant boulders. "See that hole, Martian?"

"What about it?" I asked.

"That's the reason I brought you here. This cliff has a secret."

As soon as we reached it, Solo crouched down and stuck his head inside.

"HELLO!" he yelled and his voice echoed loudly, then faded until it disappeared.

"Let me try!"

When I squatted and leaned forward I noticed that the black air inside felt much cooler.

"Hello?"

My voice wasn't as strong, but it still echoed.

Next thing I knew, Solo pulled a wooden match from his back pocket and swiped it across the rock. Cupping the flame with his other hand, he slid it through the hole as far as his arm would go.

"Hold this and look in," he said as he transferred it to my fingers.

I carefully took the match and slipped my arm and head through the hole. I couldn't believe what I saw. A cave! It was at least fifteen feet deep, and water dripped from the ceiling. It looked like the bottom of the earth.

"That's so cool!" I yelled, but my breath blew out the match. I pulled my head out. "Do you have another match?"

"Nah, but it's too late anyway to climb down in there today," said Solo. "I just wanted to bring you up here before your dad picked you up."

I was very relieved it was too late to climb down, because there was no way I wanted to actually go into a cave . . . almost as relieved as I was to miss meeting his gang of friends again. In fact, I couldn't remember feeling happier in my whole life.

"I forgot to tell you, Dad isn't picking me up," I said, "not until the end of the month. I told my parents that I want to stay."

One corner of his mouth curled up first, slowly followed by the other side. Then he picked up a rock and threw it farther than I'd ever seen him throw one. After a few seconds we heard it land in the middle of the lake.

CHAPTER TWENTY-TWO

By the time we returned to the tree house, a sea of stars sparkled in the sky. Something had changed, now that Solo knew I wouldn't be leaving for a while. He pushed me a little harder and teased me a bit more, but I didn't mind at all. Everything around us—the air, the sounds, the smells, the summer—felt lighter.

I watched as he picked up the blankets from the pile heaped in the corner and spread each one across the floor of the tree house. When he was done, six tattered covers stretched as wide as my big bed back at the house. We were about to lower the black plastic sheet over the window for the night when some flashes of light in the distance caught my attention.

"Look!" I gasped, pointing up at the mountain top. "It's that same blinking light."

Solo barely glanced as he untied the ropes.

"Wait," I said. "I want to see if there's a pattern."

"I'm telling you, it's nothing, Martian." He let the sheet of plastic unravel to the ground. "A crazy old hermit lives up there. That's all."

I had seen a movie about a hermit, but I hadn't known they actually existed. "You mean, like an old person who lives alone in the woods and never leaves?"

"Pretty much. The lights in his cabin sometimes flicker at night."

"Oh." A wave of disappointment smothered my excitement. "I thought it might be a lost hiker trying to communicate with Morse code. I brought a book that explains how to do it."

That got his attention.

"A book?" he said. "Let's read it."

Before we settled in, Solo started taking off his clothes without turning away from me. Embarrassed, I bent down and removed items from my backpack to avoid looking at him. By the time I glanced up, he was wearing nothing but his underwear.

"You brought a pillow?" he asked as I leaned it against the wall.

"Yeah. Don't you have one?"

"Nope."

He reclined on his back, his hands under his head and crossed his legs. I suddenly felt too shy to take off my clothes in front of him, so I stayed dressed in my khaki shorts and T-shirt. We lay next to each other on top of the covers since it was still hot and muggy.

I held *The Amateur's Guide to International Morse Code* with my right hand and my flashlight in my left. The first page began with information about the inventor of Morse code, who was also one of the men who invented the electric telegraph in the early eighteen hundreds.

Solo turned toward me and covered the page with his hand. "This isn't a story. These are just facts."

"But it's a book about Morse code and how to use it . . . " I tried to explain.

He flipped onto his stomach. "I don't want to hear about that, Martian. It's easy to make up a code. Don't you have any books that tell about adventures and other places far away?"

I gazed at his long spidery fingers marked with tiny scratches and scars. I could tell he chewed his fingernails, which were very pink against his dark skin.

"You said you like any book."

"Well, I like any book that's a *story*."

I closed the guide and set it down on the bare floorboards. Things weren't turning out the way I had hoped.

"Aunt Lenore has lots of books. I'll look for something else tomorrow."

I turned off the flashlight. With the window covered in black plastic, the tree house was very dark, but I could still make out slivers of glittering sky through cracks in the ceiling.

"Can you *tell* me a story?" he asked quietly.

I rolled toward him. "What kind of story?"

"Something about you and your family? About stuff you do together."

I didn't know what to say, because we really didn't do that much together other than normal things like eat dinner at the kitchen table.

"Last summer, my dad let me steer the car," I said.

He twisted back on his side. "Where were you going?"

"Out for ice cream, I think. I usually sit in the backseat, but for some reason, Dad let me sit in the front seat that day between him and my mom. We must have been celebrating something? Oh, I remember. It was my mom's birthday. She loves ice cream. Anyway, he asked me if I wanted to hold the steering wheel to see what it felt like to drive. It was wigglier than I thought it would be. And then my mom said to stop it, that it was too dangerous."

Solo didn't say anything for a minute. Then he asked, "What kind of ice cream did you get?"

"Butter pecan. That's what I always get."

"What about your parents?"

"My dad usually orders cherry vanilla, and Mom likes either mint chocolate chip or fudge ripple."

He looked away like he was thinking about something, and then he asked, "What did you do after you got ice cream?"

"Nothing, I think," I replied. "We probably went home."

It wasn't a story really, but Solo said, "Thanks, Martian," and then, "I'm glad you're staying."

With that, he rolled over onto his stomach, tucked his hands under his head, and went to sleep.

The next thing I knew, the room was bright with early morning sunshine. Solo's eyes were still closed, the bottom of his left foot pressed against my right ankle. It felt so comfortable I didn't want to move, but I had to get back to the house before Tess noticed

I was missing. As carefully as possible, I pulled my leg away from his warm foot and quietly stuffed my pillow and the book into my backpack.

After opening the trapdoor, I lowered myself down the rope ladder as it swung back and forth. About halfway down, I heard a ripping sound, and then suddenly I was falling.

I hit the ground hard on my side and yelped in pain. When I opened my eyes I saw Solo standing above me in his underpants.

"What happened? Did you slip?"

"The rope broke! And my foot really hurts."

He disappeared for a second, then returned wearing shorts. Grabbing the top half of the rope ladder, Solo climbed down as far as he could, to the point where it had snapped, and then dropped to the ground.

When he lifted my foot I winced but tried not to cry. He stood up again and examined the rope.

"I know who cut this," he said.

It hadn't occurred to me that someone would purposely sabotage the tree house.

"Why would someone cut it?"

Solo offered his hands and pulled me up. Then he gently placed my backpack over my shoulders.

"Can you walk?"

I wanted to seem brave, so I forced myself to move forward. At first the pain felt unbearable, but after a few steps it got a little better.

"I think it's okay," I said as bravely as possible.

Solo rushed over to the canoe and shoved it into the water. "Take it slowly getting back to the house, Martian."

"Wait, where are you going?"

"I need to take care of something."

Within seconds he was off, gliding across the lake. I watched until he paddled out of view. What would he need to take care of? Could it have something to do with his wild gang of friends? Or even worse, was there a rival gang out to get his gang? The thought of hordes of mean boys cutting ropes and sabotaging each other made me very nervous. Maybe Tess was right about Solo . . . about how he brought trouble and that it was better to steer clear of him.

But it was too late for that.

CHAPTER TWENTY-THREE

As I hobbled down the path toward the house, I stopped to peer in Uncle Ned's windows. I checked every single one, but he wasn't there. Everything looked organized the way it does when someone goes away—the bed made, the counters bare. Twisting on my good foot to get a view of the front room, I was relieved to see my painting of the rain still hanging over the couch.

I wondered where he went when he left, and why he seemed to leave so often. Every day on Beyond Island brought more questions, but never any answers.

Instead of following along the shoreline, I decided to take a shortcut that ran through the center of the island. Rust-colored pine needles covered the ground. I was surprised to come across a piece of trash, a clear plastic bag labeled *ONLY Market, ONLY the best,* with a red sticker on the bottom. Day-olds? I knew Solo wouldn't drop a plastic bag out in the middle of the woods. I stuffed it in my pocket to throw away later.

Like most of the paths that crisscrossed this island, this one passed through the clearing by the giant metal sculpture and Soloville. I limped over to take a look at the town, to see if any mysterious additions had been constructed overnight. As soon as I saw it, I gasped.

The entire village had been destroyed, as if someone had taken a branch and smashed it to bits.

I dropped to the ground to gather up the pieces of bark and shattered pinecones and torn blankets of moss. The side of my foot throbbed, but I barely noticed it. Who would do something so horrible to Soloville? Things were beginning to get scary around here.

I limped back to the house as fast as I could. I needed to ask Tess if she knew anything about Solo's friends and if she thought they might be after revenge. But what could Solo have done to make them so angry?

"There you are!" said Tess without looking over at me.

She was rolling white dough with a wooden rolling pin, like my mother does when she makes pie crusts on holidays.

"You're up earlier and earlier. Been down at the lake fishing? I hear the bass are biting."

I changed the subject so I wouldn't have to lie. "What are you making?"

"Shortcake. It's a bit cooler today and not so humid, so I thought I'd bake since we're loaded down in strawberries."

The moment she turned around, her mouth dropped open.

"What on earth happened to you?"

I crossed my arms and tried to stand evenly on both feet. "Nothing. Why?"

"For one thing, you're filthy," she said as she scooped steaming oatmeal into a bowl and placed it on the kitchen table. "You're never dirty. And your hair is sticking off to the side."

I had to change the subject again before she asked too many questions. "Is that oatmeal for me? It looks delicious."

"Of course it's for you. Maple syrup?"

"Yes, please," I replied and sat in my usual seat.

She continued to squint at me suspiciously another few seconds before opening the cabinet door. Then she pulled out a metal baking sheet and greased it with a slab of butter.

"Remember when you told me that Solo—I mean, Samuel—was a wild child?" I asked casually between bites.

Holding a glass upside down, she cut circles in the dough. "Yes, I do."

"What did you mean by that exactly?"

With a spatula, she scooped each white circle and transferred it onto the greased pan. After wiping her hands on her apron, she turned and leaned against the counter and studied me. "Why do you want to know, Martin?"

"It's just that—well," I stammered, "he's always telling me about his group of friends and I was thinking about maybe hanging out with them."

Tess raised her eyebrows and tilted her head. "We're talking about Samuel?"

I nodded.

"That child doesn't have a group of friends. As far as I know, he has no one."

Now I was confused. "What do you mean? He

has a whole gang of friends!"

And there it was. I had practically confessed everything I'd been trying to keep secret from her. But to my surprise, Tess wasn't upset. Instead, she slid the metal sheet filled with dough into the oven and sat across from me at the kitchen table.

"Remember what I told you when you first met Samuel?"

I tried to recall everything she'd said, besides the part about his being a wild child. "That his name wasn't Solo?"

Tess nodded. "What else?"

Then I remembered. "You said I shouldn't believe much that comes out of his mouth, and that he lives in his own world."

She patted my hand.

"I'm telling you the truth, Martin. Samuel doesn't have any friends or family to speak of, other than his cranky old great-grandfather. No one lives around these parts anymore. As I told your father, there's no work, so most families moved away years ago, especially those with children to feed. Samuel basically takes care of himself."

All at once, everything I knew about Solo felt turned upside down.

I thought about all the times he'd mentioned Clam and those other boys, but no one had ever seemed to show up.

"Why would he lie about having friends?" I asked.

Tess tilted her head and thought about it for a bit. "Maybe he needs to believe he has friends to keep from getting lonely."

That made me think of Martinville back home. My throat suddenly felt pinched. Solo pretended not to be alone, just like I did . . .

"Now do you understand what I mean when I call him a wild child?"

I nodded because I did understand, but it wasn't what I wanted to believe.

CHAPTER TWENTY-FOUR

Over the next couple of days, I didn't look for Solo and he didn't look for me.

Now that I knew a gang of boys couldn't have been involved in cutting the tree house rope, I wondered what really happened. Could Solo have set up everything to make it look as if someone else did it? And what about Soloville? Had he destroyed my town? But I couldn't think of any reason for him to do any of that.

The strangest part of all was the way he'd kept talking about his friend Clam over these past few weeks. You'd think they were inseparable the way Solo bragged about him every chance he got. Now I figured Clam had to be an imaginary friend, kind of like Mr. Little.

The problem was that no matter how hard I tried to understand Solo's situation, I still felt disappointed. He was no longer the amazing boy I'd admired so much. Now he was just a kid who lied. And maybe everything he'd helped me believe about myself was a lie too.

That was one reason I stayed put for a few days. I didn't see any point in pretending everything was still the same between Solo and me. The other reason had to do with my foot. When I finally showed my big bruise to Tess she didn't ask any questions, but she told me to soak it in the cold lake and take it easy.

So I stayed close to the house and dock, trying to keep busy. I have to admit, I was even more upset that Solo hadn't come looking for me—which was especially confusing since I wasn't even sure if I wanted to be friends with him anymore. My feelings were a tangled mess, like a bunch of charger cords stuffed in a drawer. I was even beginning to wish I had agreed to let my parents bring me home. But I had chosen to stay, so I knew I had to make the most of it.

I did small chores for Tess, and I sat and talked with Aunt Lenore a lot. I also did more reading. That's how I came across the old newspaper clipping in that poetry book for the third time—and it finally hit me.

Isaac Chambers Arrested . . .

Isaac.

Solo's great-grandfather. The one Aunt Lenore had mentioned.

No wonder Solo had stopped to look at this article. He must've recognized the picture, even though he couldn't read the words.

So Solo's great-grandfather was a criminal. Maybe Solo came from a long line of liars . . .

I read through the whole article but couldn't really understand most of it. I figured Aunt Lenore would be able to tell me more. So the next morning, after breakfast, I volunteered to bring Aunt Lenore her teapot.

"Do you mind refilling my cup too?" she asked as I placed the delicate pot on the small round table next to her rocking chair. The handle was hot, so I used the towel to pour.

"Aunt Lenore, I was wondering," I said casually. "Didn't you say Samuel's great-grandfather is named Isaac or something like that?"

"That's right," she said as she pulled the corners of her blanket to smooth out the wrinkles.

"I heard that he's some kind of criminal. Is that true?"

"Who told you that?"

"Um, I found a cut-out newspaper article up in my room . . . "

"Oh, that old business." Aunt Lenore waved a hand. "You have to understand, Martin, back then—during the Cold War years—everybody was suspicious of everybody. And people like Isaac were . . . easy targets. Many people were accused of things they hadn't done."

"But what was he even accused of?"

"It's been so long, I really don't remember the details. Antigovernment activities of some sort. The kind of charges that got thrown around a fair amount during that time."

"So he was innocent?"

"Oh, innocent's not a word I'd use to describe Isaac. He's no saint by any means. He'd as soon shoot a stranger as look at them."

"Is that why Solo doesn't live with him?"

She raised her eyebrows at me. "I assume Samuel has his reasons for everything he does. Now, would you switch on the radio on your way out? It's set to my opera station."

By the third day my foot felt a lot better, so Tess granted me my freedom again. I decided to wander over to Soloville and repair the town—and maybe rename it. Maybe by rebuilding the town, in a way, I could bring back a little order to my confused world.

More than ever I wanted nothing to do with Solo, who had lied to me and hadn't even bothered to find out if I was okay . . . But at the same time, and this was the most confusing part, I missed him a lot and felt sorry for him too.

When I reached the clearing, I was surprised to find the entire village as it had been before the attack. Not everything was exactly in the same place, but most of it was. It didn't make any sense to me. Why would Solo destroy the town only to fix it?

At that moment, something flashed through the trees. I ducked behind a bush just as someone crossed over the trail and ran toward the far side of the island. It was the same small person I had seen sneaking by the house a couple of times, dressed in dark clothes with a black hood. But now I was close enough to see he was a little kid.

Staying low, I trailed him through the woods. I remembered how fast he had been before so I raced to keep up with him. The way he silently zigzagged between thorny bushes and uneven rocks, it was as if he had grown up in the forest. Before I knew it, the lake came into view and he stopped in front of Solo's tree house. I hid behind a large stump and watched in shock as he scurried up the rope ladder, which was no longer broken, and knocked hard on the bottom of the floor. The trap door flipped opened and, instantly, I recognized Solo's thin, golden arm reach down and pull the kid inside.

It's hard to describe all the emotions I felt at that moment, but the strongest of all was a kind of crazy anger I had never experienced—so strong that it made my whole body shake and would've scared me if I'd stopped to think about it. Within seconds, I shoved the trapdoor open and barged inside the tree house, ready to demand an explanation for everything that was going on.

And then I froze.

Resting against the wall, on top of the pile of rags and blankets, was Solo, sitting next to a girl with messy blond hair.

"Hey, Martian," he said calmly as if nothing were wrong or even unusual. "This is Clam."

She glared at me, so I didn't feel as if I had to be polite and say hello.

"*Clam is a girl?*" was all I could say.

Clam immediately snuggled closer against Solo, like she owned him. And then the worst thing of all happened: Solo reached over and held her hand right in front of me!

"Of course she's a girl," he replied. "Her real name's Clementine, but I call her Clam because she doesn't like to talk. And she's really sorry about everything. Aren't you, Clam?"

She nodded, but I could tell she didn't mean it. Not one bit.

"Sorry about *what?*" I snapped back.

"You know, cutting the rope and messing up your pretend town. She was just upset that you and I were hanging out together so much."

My whole being boiled over with anger. I wanted to throw something, or hit something, or make something explode.

I didn't understand where all this emotion was coming from, but I knew I couldn't stay in that tree house one more second. I needed to get off Beyond— this confusing, infuriating island where nothing made any sense. So I slid down the rope ladder and charged directly over to Solo's canoe, pushed it into the water, climbed in, grabbed the paddle out of the bottom, and pounded the water as hard and as fast as I could.

"Hey!" he yelled from the cut-out window. "Where are you going, Martian?"

I didn't answer him. I didn't even look back.

I kept on paddling and paddling and *paddling* for as long as I could until my arms began to burn. Then my hands cramped and, just when I felt I couldn't take one more stroke, I went farther.

Until I glanced to my left and then to my right and realized I was directly in the center of the deep lake. Without a life jacket or sunscreen or anything.

And nothing looked familiar.

CHAPTER TWENTY-FIVE

To make matters much worse, a clap of thunder echoed across the mountains. I hadn't even noticed the line of dark clouds that had appeared over the far end of the lake. Now the wind was picking up and the water churned in circles like scary miniature whirlpools. For a few moments I sat paralyzed, and then I began paddling again like crazy. But the more I paddled, the less familiar everything seemed.

Another flash of light, and then a sharp *ba-bang!* Rain came pouring down in sheets of water as if the whole sky had cracked open like a giant egg. By this point it was hard for me to make out even a shadow of the shoreline. There was nothing I could do, so I shoved the paddle under my seat, buried my soaking wet head in my soaking wet hands, and bawled my eyes out. The rain pounding on my back made me feel as if the world were sobbing with me.

I wasn't even crying about being in the middle of a lake during a storm without being able to swim. The tears were for everything else I had left behind in that tree house. My feelings about Solo were so painful and now everything felt hopeless, because he didn't feel the same way about me. He liked a *girl*.

Through the wind and downpour, I heard a scratching noise and squinted through the mist. At first I thought an old rag had blown up against the boat, but after wiping my eyes with my wet sleeve, I saw it was a bird.

"Poe?"

The raven perched on the pointy front part of the canoe.

"Why are you out here in this storm?" I asked him, then sniffed and wiped my nose again.

Another lightning bolt, followed immediately by a clap of thunder almost directly overhead, made me scream. Poe lifted off and glided in two circles above me before he swooped to the left and flew away. I didn't want him to leave. I was so scared and sad and mad at the same time that I actually wanted a bird to stay with me, as if he could help me.

But then, out of the pelting rain, Poe returned and flew in two more circles. All at once, it dawned on me. He wanted me to follow him. I picked up the paddle and, just as I did, the bird swooped to the left again and flew slowly in front of the boat, his large black wings beating back the storm. If he got too far ahead he made a loop behind me so I could catch up.

Soon the rain slowed to a light steady flow and eventually a trickle, and the world started to brighten. The thunder was now a quiet rumbling far away, and I could see the shore on both sides. Along with the rain stopping, I had finished crying. All my attention had been steadied and focused by Poe, who flew farther ahead now that the skies had cleared.

"MARRRTIAN!"

Solo's distant call came from a yellow spot across the lake. Poe swooped to the right and flew in his direction. I didn't want to deal with Solo, but I didn't really have a choice. I had to follow the bird since I didn't know my way back.

"What did you do that for!?" Solo yelled at me, straddling the yellow raft. "Didn't you see that storm coming? Are you crazy? You could have been zapped!"

I stared past him and shrugged.

"What's wrong with you?" said Solo. "You're acting so weird."

I shrugged again and refused to speak. Suddenly, a wall of water hit my face.

"Stop it!" I yelled.

"I'll stop if you tell me what's going on," he said and sent another splash my way.

But instead of talking, I pulled my paddle back with all my strength and sent a huge wave in his direction, practically knocking him off the raft. Immediately, a major water fight broke out until I realized the canoe was filling up fast.

"Why didn't you tell me that Clam was *a girl?!*" I shouted as loud as I could.

"I don't know what you're talking about, Martian—obviously she's a girl!" Solo lay down on the raft to catch his breath. "Anyway, who cares? What difference does it make?"

I didn't know what to say, but in my mind, it made a *really* big difference.

"Why did she do all that mean stuff to me? What's the matter with her?"

"Nothing. She just got, you know, jealous."

I did know. I knew exactly how it felt to be jealous. "Of what?"

"I told you before," he said and sat up again. "Because you and I were hanging out and stuff. I used to spend most of my time with her."

My chest cramped and I felt sick to my stomach. Why was I reacting like this? It's not like I didn't know he had a life before I showed up. And lots of boys in my grade talked about girls all the time. But I never had any interest in it, the whole boy-girl thing.

I'm not sure why I said what I said next, except I wanted to hurt him as badly as he had hurt me . . . and I knew exactly how to do it.

"Tess told me that you don't have any real friends, that you were lying, so I guess I was surprised to find out that Clam is a real person."

He looked away and didn't say anything for a while.

"You're my real friend," he finally replied, which made me feel worse. I had to know more. "Do you like her a lot?"

Solo kicked his feet across the surface of the water. "I guess so," he said. "She's my cousin. And there's no one looking after her really, not

208

like they should. So I'm all she's got."

At that moment, every angry muscle in my body relaxed. I felt like I could breathe again.

"She's your cousin?"

He picked a stick off the raft and dropped it in the water. "Yeah. Basically. Her dad was my mom's cousin, or something like that. Anyway, her mom usually stays at the homeless shelter in the church basement with all her other kids. Clam hates it there, so she comes over to the island as much as she can. There are plenty of abandoned rowboats on the mainland that she can borrow for the day. Or she just swims across."

That's when I remembered the tiny church someone had built in Soloville, and the empty bag of day-olds in the woods, and the box of girl stuff in the tree house.

"I'm the only person she can really count on," Solo added. "She'll be okay as long as I can help her."

From the way he said it, I could tell she meant a lot to him. And now I could see why. They'd known each other a long time, maybe their whole lives. They probably understood each other better than anybody else could. Better than I ever could. "Why is she always sneaking around?" I asked.

"She has to. If Tess found out about Clam and how young she is, she would probably report us both to social services. She already worries enough about me and I can take care of myself. You won't tell her about Clam, will you?"

I tried to imagine what it would be like to have no one looking after me—no one making my meals, no one noticing if I came home or not, no one helping me when I got sick. A few weeks ago, I'd felt like my parents had abandoned me on this island, but Tess and Aunt Lenore and even Uncle Ned all cared about me. How scared and angry would I be if I had to live Clam's life?

"I won't say anything," I promised.

"Thanks. And look—you two don't have to be around each other if you don't want to be. I can just spend time with each of you on different days. I'll tell you ahead of time if I'm planning to do something with Clam."

"But how will you tell Clam if you're with me?"

"We use a code, Martian. Just like your book on codes."

"You do? How does it work?"

"We leave messages for each other with a pile of sticks at different locations. If Clam crosses two sticks next to one long stick behind Only's by the dumpster, it means she's coming over Monday. Two crossed sticks next to two long sticks means Tuesday, and so on. Or I might put three sticks, like spokes on a wheel, down by the cove. That tells Clam I'm off-island . . ."

Even though I couldn't help feeling extra jealous of their secret language, I had to admit, it was practically the coolest thing I'd ever heard of.

"So now you'll have a code for *I'm hanging out with Martin?*"

Solo nodded. "Yep. We can do that."

For some reason, that made me feel a hundred times better. We drifted in peaceful silence for another minute, the only two people on Lake Nevermore. Then Solo reached over and grabbed the back of the canoe.

"Do you wanna climb in?" I asked.

"Nope," he grinned. "I want you to tow me!"

I could barely move the boat forward, but I didn't complain. I used all my strength to paddle both of us back home.

CHAPTER TWENTY-SIX

For as long as I could remember, I'd avoided roughhousing with other boys. I'd hated playing sports and even messing around on the playground. Part of me was afraid of getting hurt, but a bigger part of me was afraid I wasn't good enough. It never felt safe to really try, so I never did. But after that day on the lake, something inside of me changed. I felt able to try almost anything, especially with Solo around.

Before I knew it, I'd learned how to skip a rock and climb a tree. (Not very far or very high, but that didn't matter.) Solo and I spent hours taking turns to see who could cast the fishing line the farthest. After dozens of tries, I even managed to drag myself up the rope into my bedroom window. And I let Solo teach me some wrestling moves in case any seventh- or eighth-graders tried to push me around in the fall.

Soon I felt stronger than I'd ever been, but I knew it wasn't just from being more active. I felt able to take risks now. I believed in myself because Solo believed in me in a way no one ever had. He didn't mind when I fell or made a mistake. He let me be *me*.

The only problem was Clam. Because they were cousins, I felt less jealous about her being close to Solo. But both of us still wanted Solo all to ourselves. For that reason alone, I knew Clam and I would never get along.

Solo warned me ahead of time when he had plans with her so that Clam and I could avoid each other, but I could tell it bothered him, and I wished things were different. There were a few times I considered spying on the cousins, but something told me to leave them alone. So instead, when they were together, I worked on Soloville, did extra chores, kept Aunt Lenore company, or skimmed through the books in the den . . . and tried very hard not to think about Solo and Clam.

One afternoon, when I randomly picked up a dusty old book with *The Poems of Edgar Allan Poe* printed across the cover, Aunt Lenore suddenly stopped rocking in her chair. Then she blinked her enormous owl eyes several times and beckoned me to move closer.

"Ah, you've found our origin story."

"Your what?"

"My father loved Poe's works. It's half the reason he wanted to buy property on Lake Nevermore— *nevermore* is one of Poe's favorite words, you know. And I'm named after one of Poe's most famous characters. My brother's given name is Edgar, but he never could stand it, so he's always gone by the nickname, Ned."

"Wait—so that's where the bird's name comes from?"

"Yes. My father started the tradition of keeping pet ravens too. He was a bit—shall we say—obsessive. I happen to like ravens, but I can't say I'm a great admirer of Poe the writer. He seemed so stuck."

"Stuck?"

"Stuck in the past, brooding over his losses. Afraid to move forward. It makes for quite depressing reading. Take my advice, Martin—don't turn into that kind of person. My father did. Goodness knows, I have too. Don't ever let disappointment and fear stop you from living a full life."

She rocked the chair a couple of times and closed her eyes again. I wondered why Aunt Lenore felt the need to tell me all this. It was as if she knew about my dilemma with Solo and Clam, about how upset I'd been. But of course she hadn't been talking about that. She'd been talking about her weird family. Which I guess, technically, I was part of.

The thought of family made me remember my dad—for the first time in what seemed like forever. I wondered what would happen to the island if he actually inherited it and then sold it. Would somebody tear down this house and build some fancy new mansion? Would the whole place get turned into some kind of resort filled with people who "didn't respect the island" either? The thought made me feel a little sick to my stomach.

Later that evening, Tess said, "Martin, I need to take Lenore to the mainland for her doctor's appointment tomorrow afternoon."

"Oh, okay." I figured it was probably a good idea for an old person to visit the doctor regularly. Though I had to wonder how much longer Aunt

Lenore was going to fake her forgetfulness.

But Tess wasn't finished. "The trip to Augusta and back is too much for Lenore to do in one day. So I've reserved a hotel room for the night. Would you mind staying here at the house and keeping an eye on Lenore's bird? She worries about him. And we really shouldn't skip a day of weeding the garden either."

Never in a million years would my parents have left me by myself for a whole night. I wasn't sure if I liked the idea or not.

"Will Uncle Ned be in his cabin?"

"It doesn't look like it," she sighed. "He was supposed to be back by now . . . but you shouldn't need anything from him while we're gone."

The way Tess asked me, as if she had no concerns about leaving me to be in charge all on my own, gave me the confidence I needed. Plus—a whole day with nobody on the island except Solo and me? That thought pushed out the last of my worries.

It's not as if Tess or Aunt Lenore or Uncle Ned bothered me in any way. Other than my mom, they were pretty much the nicest adults I'd ever met. But no matter how much you liked a grown-up, they were always in charge. So having the whole island to ourselves would mean it was *our* island, where we could do anything we wanted to do.

Early the next morning I couldn't wait to tell Solo the news, but he wasn't as excited as I'd hoped he'd be. And when I asked him if he wanted to spend the night at the big house with me—even though I knew Tess didn't exactly approve of his wild ways—to my surprise, he said he'd prefer we slept in the tree house.

Of course, it wouldn't exactly be comfortable lying on that hard floor with a pile of rags for covers. But the tree house was still one of my favorite places on the island, so I agreed.

A couple hours later, Tess and Aunt Lenore were packed, dressed, and ready for their trip. They stood by the counter arguing over a checklist as I entered the kitchen to see how things were going.

"You don't need three necklaces for a one-night trip," insisted Tess.

"But what if the governor invites us to stay at the mansion?" Aunt Lenore squawked, then turned to me and winked.

I had to cover my mouth so I wouldn't laugh. I had to admit, Aunt Lenore's fake craziness could be funny at times. Though I also felt a little sorry for Tess, since she thought it was real.

"Why don't you visit the bathroom one more time before we cross," said Tess. "Since Ned isn't back, I've arranged to have us picked up at the dock. Mr. Eames from the village will row out to get us, and the limo will be waiting on the other side."

"But I don't need the bathroom," Aunt Lenore replied.

"Maybe you should check your hair?"

Aunt Lenore clutched the top of her head, then hurried down the hall.

"Wow," I said. "You're taking a limo to the doctor's office?"

"It's really just a neighbor," whispered Tess. "I hire him to drive us when we need to get somewhere. He has a black car that Lenore believes is a limousine, which is just fine with me if it makes her happy."

I didn't say anything, since Aunt Lenore was counting on me to keep her weird secret.

Tess reviewed everything one more time. "There's plenty of food in the fridge, including a pheasant potpie for dinner. Feel free to give Poe a few scraps if he starts tapping at the back door for food. Oh, I almost forgot, I think the phone's gone out again—I tried to call Mr. Eames this morning to confirm our pickup and couldn't get a dial tone. So if there's an emergency, Samuel can get you off the island and into town where you can make a call. I'll get someone out here to look at the phone once we're back . . ."

"*Tessss?*" Aunt Lenore's voice carried down the hall. "Where's my lavender perfume? The one the duke complimented at the charity ball last May? "

Tess rolled her eyes. "*Coming!*" she called back. "Now most important, Martin, use your common sense. Don't let Samuel talk you into doing anything crazy. Get to bed early and promise me you'll behave like a responsible young man?"

"Promise!" I said, and I meant it.

CHAPTER TWENTY-SEVEN

As soon as the neighbor's rowboat disappeared from sight, I ran from the dock to the tree house as fast as I could. "Hoot-hoot!" I called.

In the distance, I heard a faint, "Caw-caw."

I waited a few seconds before calling again. "HOOT-HOOT!"

The reply came a little louder this time. "*Caw-caw.*"

I raced away from the tree house to follow the sound. Each time I hooted, a few seconds later Solo cawed. This went on for several minutes as we crept around the woods, each of us trying to catch the other one first.

"Got you!"

Solo grabbed me from behind, squeezed my middle with his arms, and lifted me off the ground. Then we both fell down onto our backs laughing until we couldn't laugh anymore and stared up at the sky. Through a gap in the trees we could see puffy clouds.

"I see a rabbit," I said, pointing to the right.

"A rabbit?" said Solo. "That's a moose. A male one—see the antlers?"

After that we made slingshots, which Solo had taught me to do one night up in the tree house. All it took was a Y-shaped branch, a rubber band, and a knife. Solo's aim was so accurate he could knock a leaf off a bush. He said the trick was to concentrate on lining up the stick and not worrying about where the elastic was pointing. We set up targets all over the island and made up a game to see who could race through the course and hit all the targets faster. Five seconds were added to your score for every target you missed.

We began to lose track of points, so we took off our shirts and marked our arms with berry juice to keep score. I liked the way the lines of berry stains made it look as if we had tattoos. After playing a bunch of times, we almost tied, although I'm not sure Solo was trying as hard as he could. By the end, our whole bodies were covered in berry juice stripes.

We got so hot that we raced each other through the woods over to the lake, but as usual, I stopped before the water rose above my waist. Solo instantly dove in and disappeared. I still wasn't used to the long time he held his breath and stayed under. And I always got ten times more nervous during the last few seconds before he burst to the surface.

"Come on in, Martian!"

"Okay, but I need to go upstairs and get my life vest."

"No vest," he called and swam over to me. "Try floating right here. I'll help."

I groaned like always. "You know I can't!"

The one exception to my newfound confidence was swimming. I still refused to try, at least not without the life vest. Since I knew I couldn't float, I was convinced I would drown.

After bending his knees until the water reached his chest, Solo spread his arms out, tilted his head back, then lifted his legs until he was floating as effortlessly as lying on a bed.

He stood up again. "Do exactly what I did," he explained. "It's shallow here. Nothing will happen."

Each time he showed me, he made it look easier, and I wanted to do it more than anything else. After pulling in a deep breath, I bent my knees and tried. But I didn't squat far enough into the water, so my head plopped backward before I could spread my arms.

Solo patted my back as I coughed and gagged.

"Try again," he said.

"Do I have to?"

"You almost got it."

This time he put his hand on my back before I began and kept it there, which gave me the courage I needed to try one more time. I bent my knees as far as I could until the water was up to my neck, and I slowly pushed my arms to my sides as I leaned my head back against the soft water. Solo pressed my lower back to help lift my legs and with his other hand he scooped under my knees and held me. For a brief few seconds I felt completely relaxed and happy. I was floating! Until Solo suddenly pulled away both hands and I sank.

This time I coughed so much I almost threw up.

"You're getting it!" he said as I stumbled out of the lake and collapsed in the weeds.

He rushed to my side and stood over me. Water from his wet hair dripped on my body.

"Why did you let go?" I moaned.

"So you could float on your own, Martian." He tapped my leg with his foot. "It doesn't count if I'm holding you."

Neither of us said anything until he tapped me again. "Try one more time?"

I shook my head. Even with Solo encouraging me, I knew this was something I'd never be able to learn.

"Never again. I can't do it."

The sun was directly overhead, which meant it was time for lunch. But I had a hard time convincing Solo to make a sandwich with me in the kitchen.

"I don't need anyone else's food," he insisted.

"I know you don't *need* it," I explained, "but Tess left it here to be eaten, so why waste it?"

It turned out Solo was starving. Or, at least, he appeared to be starving. I put everything we could possibly eat for lunch on the kitchen table, and his eyes popped out of his head. The first thing he went for was the ham, which he layered with slabs of cheese and devoured with a buttered roll. Eventually he moved on to cold carrot soup, a bowl of strawberries, and a glass of milk. I opted for my usual peanut butter and honey on toast.

"Why don't you ever eat here at the house?"

"I told you," he said quietly, "I have my own food."

I knew by now that Solo preferred not to answer direct questions—that I would have to wait until he wanted to explain it to me. I guess it had to be difficult for him to trust anyone other than himself, and I kind of knew how that felt.

After lunch we were both sleepy from eating too much, so I suggested we look for a book in the den, even though everything we had tried to read so far had been boring, old, and smelly.

"How about this?" Solo asked, lifting a thick novel off the shelf.

"*The Adventures of Tom Sawyer*," I read aloud. I had heard of Tom Sawyer, but it definitely didn't sound like something I would ever want to read.

"Sounds great!" said Solo.

We took the book down to the dock. I lay on my stomach, propped up on my elbows, while Solo reclined on his back and listened. As soon as I read the first pages of the first chapter I knew this story would be old-fashioned, written in a way that I could barely understand, like so many of Aunt

Lenore's books. I closed it and sighed.

Solo turned his head toward me. "Keep reading, Martian."

"Why? It's huge, and I already have no idea what's going on. I wish we could find a book written in normal English."

"What are you talking about? That kid Tom gets in trouble right away and then takes off. I wanna know what happens to him!"

I sat up and looked down at Solo. "How did you figure that out?"

"Because that's what it says."

That's when it occurred to me that maybe he actually understood what was going on in all these strange old books. So I had an idea.

"Why don't I teach you how to read? Then you can read whatever and whenever you want all year long."

The sun was behind my head, so Solo had to squint hard as he looked up at me. "There's no point," he mumbled. "I know the letters—I just can't put them together."

I had never heard of anyone with that problem before, but I thought about how frustrating it must be. It reminded me of my failure to float. I was missing out on a whole world of swimming in the same way Solo was left out of the world of reading.

Because I knew exactly how it felt, I knew not to push him and went back to reading the book. And after a while I started to like it a little. The thing is, I never would have understood the story if I hadn't stopped at the end of each chapter for Solo to explain. It was as if he already knew what was going to happen, the same way he seemed to know how to do almost anything.

After about an hour of following all the trouble caused by that kid, Tom Sawyer, something stung the middle of my spine so sharply I jumped to my feet.

"Ouch! What was that?"

Solo checked my back. "Maybe a bug bite?" he asked.

I turned in circles looking for a wasp or a bee or whatever it was that got me, and that's when I saw her. Clam was sitting on a large boulder by the shore, holding one of our slingshots in her hand.

CHAPTER TWENTY-EIGHT

"Apologize to Martian," said Solo.

Clam stood next to him, her messy yellow hair hanging like a shredded curtain across her face. She must have known the adults were gone, because she wasn't wearing her usual disguise. Instead she wore a ratty T-shirt and long shorts, pretty much what Solo wore every day.

She whispered something and Solo nudged her. "I know you don't like to talk, Clam," he said, "but it's just one word."

Her fists were clenched by her sides. "Sorry," she whispered, barely loud enough to hear.

Solo reached for her hand, and instantly I felt jealous.

"She told me she was sad when she saw the message I left for her behind Only's."

"Why? What did your message say?" I asked.

"That I would be busy with you for a couple more days."

The breeze blew Clam's tangled hair away from her face. I could see red scratches on her cheek.

"Then why did she come?"

I knew it was wrong, but I felt no sympathy for this girl who constantly took Solo's attention away from me. All I felt was anger toward her for ruining my perfect afternoon.

Solo didn't answer me. Clam leaned against him and I could see his hand tighten around hers.

"Could she stay awhile, Martian?" he asked. "She'll go back before it gets dark."

Now I was furious. Didn't he know having Clam here changed everything?

"I'm leaving in a week," I reminded him, glaring at Clam, who refused to look me in the eye. "After that, you two can be together *all the time*."

I could tell Solo was disappointed and didn't know what to do. Then suddenly the messy little girl released his hand and ran away. To my surprise, he didn't follow her or even call out her name as she scrambled over bushes and rocks until we could no longer see her.

Solo sat down on the edge of the dock and dropped his feet into the lake. Everything felt different again, just as it had the moment I discovered the two of them in the tree house. I knew I shouldn't be so mean to Clam and that I shouldn't make Solo feel as if he had to choose between us, but it was as if I had no control over what I said or felt. I had never behaved like this before with anyone in my entire life.

It was more than wanting Solo all to myself. I also wanted him to like me more than anyone else.

"Wanna keep reading?" I asked as I sat next to him.

Normally I didn't dangle my feet off the dock because I didn't want the fish to mistake my toes for bait, but this time I made an exception.

"Nah."

We didn't say anything for a very long time. It's interesting what you can hear when you're awkwardly silent on a quiet island on a still lake on a hot afternoon where there are no boats or cars or the everyday hum of people. First you notice how loud the insects can be. Then the birds chime in, chirping up a storm as the chipmunks chatter below in the brush. In the background, the constant breeze rustles through the trees and water laps at the dock. Eventually, you can hear your own heartbeat.

"I didn't know you were leaving so soon, Martian."

Solo leaned over the lake and made circles in the water with his feet. A surge of happiness returned.

"I'm only here for July, and it'll be August next week." After a moment I added, "I really wish I could stay the whole summer."

Until now, I hadn't allowed myself to think about leaving. I couldn't even imagine what life would be like once I got back to Delaware. Nothing would ever be the same again.

Suddenly, Solo popped up.

"Then we better not waste time," he said as he shook off his feet. "Beat you to the cove!"

Although I'd stopped worrying as much about trying new things or pushing myself to see what I could do, there were still times when I knew I was too far outside my comfort zone and had to say no. Now was one of those times.

Solo was chasing a slimy green frog through the mud. He caught one of its long legs for a second before it leapt into the safety of a bush. "You need to catch two, Martian, one for each hand," he explained and tried to grab another.

"I don't know." I cringed. "I don't think the frog would enjoy that . . . "

Solo stood up and wiped his hands down the front of his shorts, leaving streaks of dirt. "How would you know? Maybe they like racing each other."

Whether or not they liked it, I knew I didn't like it, not one bit. "Since it's my last week, can't we do something else?"

I knew exactly what I wanted to do, something we hadn't done together since the first day we met.

I half expected Soloville to be in shambles after I scared Clam away, but luckily everything was still in one piece. Solo couldn't think of anything to build since I vetoed gloomy places like a graveyard or a jail or a dump.

"Why don't you build a miniature tree house?"

Immediately he began gathering supplies, starting with a fat twig which he used as a pine tree. We worked side by side for a long time, speaking to each other only when we needed materials like a leaf or a smooth stone. As Solo worked on the tree house, I made all the finishing touches, arranging tiny gardens and stop signs. Finally, we took a step back to admire our work.

"So who lives here, Martian?"

"We do," I said as if it could be true. I had finally ended up exactly where I wanted to be . . . living with my best friend in the best place in the whole world.

"Then we need to give our town a name," said Solo.

I grinned from ear to ear, but wasn't sure I should tell him, not yet. Just then, a breeze blew through the clearing and a loud whistling filled the air. "What's that noise?"

"Just the blob," he said as he glanced over at the towering sculpture. "The screws are always coming loose."

"Why do you call it *the blob?*"

"What else would you call it?"

The whistling grew louder as the wind picked up. I followed Solo across the clearing and watched as he found the exact screw making the noise and tightened it with his fingers. Instantly, the whistling stopped.

"I don't think it's a blob," I said as the spinners spun in silence. "I like it. Uncle Ned told me his friend made it."

But Solo didn't reply as he moved among the metal pieces, stopping to tighten and adjust various parts, as if he had built it himself.

After eating Tess's pheasant potpie for dinner, we cleaned up and turned on the porch light before heading over to the tree house for the night. I looked around for Poe, but I hadn't seen him all day. Solo ran ahead to start the fire while I packed my pillow, our book, and a couple other things. As I turned off the lights in the upstairs hallway, I heard noises coming from one of the empty bedrooms—not the usual creaking, more like something opening and closing.

"Hello?" I called out, but heard nothing.

Though I'd grown used to the spooky sounds of that old house, I was very glad not to be spending the night alone in my bedroom, and I took off across the island as fast as I could.

Solo was reclining against a rock by a small fire at the water's edge when I slid to a stop in front of him, huffing and puffing. A million stars and a half moon lit the sky. I bent over to catch my breath.

"What happened to you? Did you see a ghost?"

"No," I replied between breaths, "but I think I heard one."

Solo laughed. "You crack me up, Martian."

He handed me a small branch with a pointy end, then reached into a bag of marshmallows (stamped with Only's red sticker) and slid one onto his stick. I decided day-old old marshmallows from the top of the dumpster couldn't make me sick once I cooked them over the fire. A light breeze kept the bugs away. There was no need to say a word. It was a perfect night.

Once we settled under the covers up in the tree house, I continued to read *The Adventures of Tom Sawyer*. We picked up where Tom meets a kid named Huckleberry Finn, who reminded me of Solo. Although I didn't think I should mention the resemblance, since Huck, unlike Solo, had some negative qualities. But I noticed Solo seemed to be listening even more closely than before, so I wondered if he was thinking the same thing. He leaned on his side, just inches from my right ear, and every time I tried to stop he begged me to read one more page. Finally, he rolled onto his back. I put the book down and turned off my flashlight.

"Martian?"

I turned toward him but could barely make out the outline of his body.

"Thanks for reading."

I smiled even though I knew he couldn't see me. "You're welcome."

After several seconds he added, "I used to have lots of friends when I was in school."

I thought about that and knew it had to be true. I was sure everyone who ever met Solo wanted to be his friend.

"It's the opposite for me," I told him. "I don't have any friends at school. No real friends. Not like you."

He turned over onto his stomach and yawned. "You will, Martian, just wait and see."

But I didn't want to think about school or home or anywhere else on the planet. I wanted to stay on Beyond Island forever.

In the early hours of the morning a tapping noise woke me. I went to the window and ducked my head under the black plastic sheet to take a look outside. The sun had just begun to appear over the horizon, but the sky above was still dark. I could make out the shape of a large bird standing at the end of a branch.

"Poe? Is that you?"

He bounced across the tree until he was practically within my reach, then turned and took flight over the lake. I watched until he faded into the haze. It took me a minute to realize Poe was flying directly toward a faint flashing light. The same flashing light I had seen coming from the hermit's cabin at the top of the mountain.

Almost instantly, I recognized the pattern.

Dot–dot–dot.

Space–space–space.

Dot–dot–dot.

SOS.

CHAPTER TWENTY-NINE

I rushed over to Solo and shook him awake.

"I was right! It's Morse code!" I cried. "And they're sending the distress signal. SOS! Someone needs help!"

Solo sat up and stretched. "What are you talking about, Martian?"

"The lights! Poe saw it and he woke me up!"

I dragged him over to the window and whipped the sheet of plastic over our heads, but I didn't have to point. Solo knew exactly where to look.

The pattern continued to blink over and over again from the top of the peak.

"Help," he said softly. "That means help."

"That's what I just told you!" I yelled. "Shouldn't we call 9-1-1?"

Without saying a word, Solo pulled on his clothes and an old pair of sneakers he rarely wore.

"We can go back to the house," I said, "and use the phone to call . . ." Then I remembered the phone was out. But Uncle Ned's cabin had a phone too, so maybe if we could get in there somehow . . .

Solo shook his head impatiently. "There aren't any roads up that mountain—not any real roads, nothing big enough for a car or an ambulance. It won't do any good to call the mainland."

"Then what can we do?"

"I'm going up."

"What?! *You're* going to help? By yourself?"

I had never seen him act like this.

"Have to. Something must be really wrong. He only uses that signal when it's an emergency."

"Who are you talking about? The old hermit?"

He flipped open the trapdoor and grabbed the rope ladder.

"Yeah, Isaac. My great-grandfather."

Within a few minutes, I managed to get dressed and run over to the edge of the lake, where the canoe was still wedged under a bush. A moment later Solo appeared, running down the trail toward me.

"Where did you go?" I asked.

He patted his stuffed pockets. "I needed to get supplies."

"For the hermit—I mean, your great-grandfather?"

"No, probably not for him."

None of this was making sense. But I knew now wasn't the time for explanations. On a low rock near the water, Solo quickly arranged a bunch of sticks. I didn't have to ask: a message for Clam. Then he slipped into the back seat of the canoe.

"Wait!" I cried. "I'll come too. It'll be faster with two people." I wasn't sure this was actually true—since I'd also be adding more weight to the boat—but I couldn't stand the thought of being left behind and just wondering what was happening.

"Are you sure, Martian?" he asked. "You don't have your life vest."

Without hesitating, I grabbed the front of the canoe, threw my sneakers in, and sat on the front seat. I wanted to help Solo more than anything in the world. Nothing else mattered. I picked up the second paddle and pushed off against the bottom of the lake.

We glided through the water faster than we ever

had before, as if we were sliding across glass, dipping our paddles in perfect rhythm. Minutes later, as the sun peeked over the horizon, we reached the mainland. Two deer, a mother and a baby, dashed away when we landed the boat. Together we slid the canoe beneath a bush, not far from an old metal rowboat tied to a tree. I wondered who else could be here this early in the morning on a remote part of the lake.

"Thanks, Martian. Maybe you should wait here till I get back?"

"No way," I said. "I'm going with you."

"Listen, I need to move fast. And it's not an easy climb."

"Then you shouldn't go by yourself." I didn't say it, but I was thinking that Solo shouldn't be going alone to meet a crazy hermit criminal—even if that crazy hermit criminal was his great-grandfather.

"I'll be fine."

"Come on, I'm not gonna stay down here doing nothing," I said. "Let's just go, we're wasting time."

Solo didn't bother to keep arguing with me. He hurried toward an opening in the dense forest and then started up a narrow trail, with me following close behind. To keep up, I watched the ground so I wouldn't slip or trip. Soon the path grew very steep, winding through pine trees and thick scratchy bushes. Several times the trail forked in different directions. If I had been alone I would've quickly lost my way, but it was clear Solo knew exactly where he was going.

After an hour or so, the trees almost disappeared and now the bright sunshine beat down on our heads. I had never felt so tired in my whole life, and I was starting to fall behind. Solo glanced back, then stopped and told me to take a break. As soon as I lifted my focus from the ground I saw the view: Lake Nevermore from one end to the other.

"Over there is Aidenn," said Solo, pointing to the left in the far northern corner, "and that dot in the middle is Beyond."

For an island filled with so many undiscovered corners, it looked very small from this distance.

I wiped the sweat off my forehead with the bottom of my shirt. "I'm thirsty," I said. "I wish we had water."

"There's a stream farther up."

I remembered what Tess had told me about drinking only from the tap. "Is it safe?"

"The water's from an underground brook," he said. "I drink from it all the time."

Soon I could hear the sound of a rushing stream. I was so thirsty, I had no choice but to trust Solo. We squatted in front of a large, smooth rock where he said the water would be cleanest and cupped our hands under the steady flow. I gulped down as much as I could, then stuck my whole face into the ice-cold water.

Feeling refreshed, we both had a burst of energy as we continued along the trail, but when I looked up, the mountain seemed to go on forever. What if Solo had been right to doubt me—what if I couldn't make it to the top? The sun was now high enough in the sky to drench us in sweat. We both pulled off our shirts and wrapped them around our heads, like turbans, to help shade our eyes. Solo still had bright purple berry stripes across his arms and body from yesterday's slingshot game. Mine had faded more than his. We grabbed handfuls of ferns to swat away the bugs.

Soon my stomach began to growl, telling me it was way past oatmeal and syrup time in the kitchen, even though I had no idea how to cook it myself. Tess had suggested I make toast, which also sounded delicious right about now.

"Did you bring any food?" I asked.

I had noticed Solo's bulging pockets, but until now I hadn't thought about what he had meant by "supplies."

He shook his head. "Nope, but we'll get some at the cabin."

"So what's stuffed in your pockets if it's not food?"

"Medicine bottles. I'm not sure what they're going to need when we get there."

"They? I thought you said he was a hermit."

Solo didn't answer, as if he wasn't sure he should.

"Is your great-grandfather in trouble? Is he hiding out at the top of the mountain?"

"He's not exactly hiding out. It'll be easier to explain when we get there."

The hot sun on my head combined with hunger pains was starting to make me dizzy. I didn't want to slow Solo down, so I forced myself forward. At times the trail dipped into trees bringing cool shade, but as soon as we hit a sunny clearing, I felt light-headed again. I started to count my steps to distract myself, but Solo moved so quickly it was hard to concentrate.

Every bone in my body ached and my head throbbed, but somehow I put one foot in front of the other. Together we moved silently forward. I copied every step Solo took, bent over like a hundred-year-old man and staring down at the backs of his feet. Suddenly, he stopped and I bumped against him.

"Hey, why are we—"

Solo grabbed my arm and squeezed so hard I instantly knew something was wrong. I leaned to one side. Barely thirty feet away, to the right of the trail, stood a gigantic moose.

Or what I assumed to be a moose, since I had only seen them on TV. It was, by far, the biggest animal I'd ever been this close to outside of a zoo. Its legs were taller than my whole body, and it had those enormous pointy antlers. *The antlers mean it's a male*, I thought, right before the moose threw his huge head back and made an angry grunting noise.

Solo whispered, "Back. Up. Slowly."

I had to force my legs to move. The moose grunted more loudly and stomped the ground with his front foot. He seemed to be glaring at us.

"I'm going to charge him," Solo continued, "and I want you to run past and up the path toward the cabin. Get help."

"*What?!*"

"Just do it. NOW!"

And then Solo ran straight toward the massive

grunting creature, yelling at the top of his lungs. I was right behind him until I veered off to the left and up the path.

Solo couldn't fend off that animal for long. And I was the only one who could get help. I knew I had to locate that scary old hermit as fast as possible.

CHAPTER THIRTY

I raced up and up and up the trail until I couldn't hear Solo shouting anymore. I was so exhausted I had to stop for a second. And that's when I caught a glimpse of a shiny metal roof through the pine trees. The sky had opened up. The top! I was near the top!

But then, out of nowhere, a gunshot cracked through the air.

I dropped to the ground just like they do in the movies. I had never heard a gun in real life, and it sounded a hundred times more frightening than I'd ever imagined.

A second gunshot! The crazy hermit criminal was shooting—at *me*.

"*Don't kill me!*" I screamed as loud as I could. My

entire body shook so hard I could barely manage to crawl behind the nearest large rock. How could so many horrible things be happening at once?!

Then I thought of Solo, trying to fend off that huge angry moose all by himself. I *had* to get help for him.

To help myself calm down, I dragged my shirt down off my head and over my trembling body. The shots seemed to have stopped, so I forced myself to peer around the edge of the rock. A grisly old man held a walking stick with his right hand and pointed a rifle with his left.

"Samuel?" he hollered down the hill toward me. "That you? I thought you were a coon after my hens again."

It took every last ounce of my strength and courage to stand up, step out, and speak.

"I'm his friend! He needs HELP!"

The old man took a few steps forward. "What's that? Who are you?"

"*Please!*" I cried out and ran toward him. "A moose is trying to kill him!"

As scared as I was, somehow I managed to grab his sleeve near his elbow—the same arm that held the gun—and drag the old man forward. "This way!"

As I led the hermit down the trail, I could hear Solo yelling again, in between awful pounding noises and growling grunts. All at once, I couldn't stop myself from breaking into a full run. I'm not sure what I was thinking, other than that I couldn't leave Solo alone. But as soon I saw the situation, I stopped in my tracks. Solo was clinging to the top of a shaking tree, and the moose was ramming the trunk with his antlers.

Another gunshot rang out.

"*Skedaddle!*" the old man bellowed and fired up into the air two more times.

The moose glanced back at us with the angriest eyes I'd ever seen. White foam frothed all around his mouth. Solo's great-grandfather breathed heavily as he caught up to me. He placed his heavy hand on my shoulder.

"Stay still," he said, but he didn't have to tell me that. I wasn't going anywhere.

And then just like that, as if nothing horrifying had just taken place, the gigantic creature turned and silently disappeared into the forest.

I looked up at Solo, who was still clinging to the top of the tree. I wanted to rush over, but the old man held my shoulder.

"Hang on. Need to make sure that big fella is long gone."

We waited only a minute or two, but it seemed more like an hour.

Then the old man laughed a deep roaring laugh. From the top of the tree, Solo began to laugh too. And before I knew it I was laughing with them. I laughed so hard I collapsed onto the ground and exploded with laughter until my stomach ached and tears streamed down the sides of my head.

"You saved my life, Martian."

I wiped my face with the back of my hands and sat up. Solo was standing over me, the sky beyond him bluer than I remember ever seeing it. He reached down and I reached up.

CHAPTER THIRTY-ONE

"I need to get back," said Solo's great-grandfather. "You got the medicine?"

Solo reached into his pockets and handed over some plastic pill bottles. His great-grandfather nodded. "You done a good thing, kid." He stuffed the bottles into his shirt, then turned and hurried back up the trail. He leaned on the walking stick with one hand while using the other to grip the rifle, which rested against his shoulder. He didn't look sick, at least not emergency-room sick, but he was very old and I knew some old people needed to take a lot of pills.

Solo patted my back and smiled. "Are you okay, Martian?"

"Of course I'm okay," I said as I wiped my eyes again, trying to hide the fact that the scariest, craziest experience of my entire life had just taken place. "Are *you* okay? That moose almost killed you!"

"I knew you'd get help," he said. "And Isaac's always carrying that rifle around, shooting off warning shots at the world."

We moved very slowly, both of us shaken and exhausted. By now it was about noon, and the sun was high in the sky. Finally I saw the shiny roof through the trees again, but also tiny flashes of blinding light. At first I thought the flashes were spots in my eyes, a sign that I was getting lightheaded again—until we turned to the right. Two tall stone posts formed an entranceway, and I couldn't believe what I saw beyond them.

Sculptures, like the one in the clearing on the island, were everywhere. Big and small, tall and short, made of junk metal, stone, chunks of wood, glass bottles—they filled the open space around the hermit's square log cabin. Hundreds of moving parts caught the sunlight as they twirled. It was a spectacular sight.

"Come on, Martian," said Solo as he walked ahead toward the cabin. But I couldn't stop staring.

I wandered through the towering maze, studying every single one.

And beyond the sculptures was the unbelievable view. I could see all of Lake Nevermore, plus other lakes and ponds and rivers in the distance. A long line of mountaintops continued as far as the eye could see. Down the hill, behind a wire fence, goats grazed near a small barn. A weird feeling came over me, as if I had been here before, but I didn't know how that was possible. Why did it all feel so familiar?

"This place is *incredible*," I said out loud to myself.

Suddenly the cabin door slammed shut. The old man, leaning on his cane, stood on the front porch next to Solo. Now I noticed that his gray hair grew over his ears and his bushy white beard had black stripes, pretty much the way I'd imagined a hermit would look.

"Who is this kid anyway?" he asked Solo.

"The boy from Beyond," I heard Solo say. "He wanted to come."

The old man walked down the steps and stared at me. I'm sure I seemed as odd to him as he did to me. "You might as well come inside."

Climbing up the steps, I noticed the shotgun at the end of the porch and shuddered. I had never really seen one up close—and to think, I had already heard it go off five times. It just didn't make sense to me that a terrifying gun and a field of amazing sculptures could be owned by the same man.

The inside of his house contained more recycled materials—furniture made from scraps, from sawed-off logs, from window panes. But none of it looked like junk. It was all strangely beautiful.

Solo filled two glasses with water from the sink, and I drank mine down in one long chug. Isaac continued to squint suspiciously at me, which made him seem even scarier.

"You boys hungry?" he grunted.

We sat at a round table made of mismatched colorful tiles and watched as he cracked a bunch of eggs into a black frying pan sizzling with oil. While the eggs cooked, he made toast. None of us said a word.

When Isaac placed the plates on the table I noticed his hands were massive, like a giant's hands. Then he collapsed in the rocking chair as if making eggs was the most tiring thing in the world. No wonder he never left this mountain. He would never make it back up.

The moment Solo lifted his fork I dove in and gobbled down the food.

"I suppose you find it amusing, meeting the world-famous hermit?" said the old man. "Now you can run into Only's and tell all the folks you saw him!"

I had no idea how to respond to that comment.

"The crazy lawless sculptor at the top of the mountain," he muttered. "The one accused of *treason!*"

"He isn't from around here, Isaac," said Solo. "He doesn't care about all that. He's just visiting."

His great-grandfather rocked hard in his chair as I silently sliced the crusts off my toast.

"None of it was true," he went on. "Not a bit of it. I would have fought in the war if I could have. Born deaf in my right ear, can't help that."

I nodded, not sure what to say.

He pounded his walking stick on the floor and burst out, "Why can't people leave you in peace?"

I glanced at Solo, who was still eating as if nothing weird was happening. I let my eyes wander around the room. It seemed impossible that this raging, bitter person could have anything to do with the magic inside this house.

Just then a moaning sound came from another room.

"What was that?" I blurted. The person was obviously in pain.

The hermit swore under his breath. "Must have disturbed him."

"Is he okay?" asked Solo.

"He will be as soon as the medicine takes hold."

My imagination ran wild wondering who was on the other side of that door. This cabin was the perfect place for a criminal to hold someone hostage. I could feel the goosebumps rising all over my body.

But then a soft, low voice came from the other room.

"*Isaac?*"

Solo's great-grandfather grabbed his stick and struggled to stand before he replied.

"Be right there, Ned."

CHAPTER THIRTY-TWO

It turned out the emergency had been Uncle Ned, who needed special medicine that he had forgotten back on the island. When Solo got the SOS, he knew to gather every prescription bottle he could find in Ned's cabin, because the same emergency had happened before.

"But I don't get why Uncle Ned is here in the first place," I said to Solo.

Solo shrugged. "He's always here, when he isn't on Beyond."

"You mean, this is where he goes when he goes away?"

Solo nodded.

"But why?" I asked. "Do they have a business together making the sculptures?"

That made Solo laugh. "Who would pay anything for those blobs?"

"I would, if I had the money to buy one."

Solo made a face like he was sucking on a lemon. "Isaac wouldn't sell them anyway," he mumbled.

We could hear the murmurings of the two men's voices in the other room. I wondered what they could be saying and tried to listen. Solo wandered over to the kitchen and searched through the cabinets. He shook something into his hand.

"Want some sunflower seeds?" He popped one in his mouth, cracked the shell with his teeth, then spit the remains into the sink.

"No thanks."

I stood up and gazed at the field of metal sculptures through the kitchen window. If I let them, the flashing, spinning parts could hypnotize me.

"Did your great-grandfather make all these himself?"

"Mostly," said Solo. "Ned helps more now, since it's getting hard for Isaac to build them alone."

Even though this place was astonishing, I still didn't understand why Uncle Ned bothered to hike all the way up the mountain just to spend time with a crabby old loner.

"So are they old friends or what?" I turned back and looked directly at him. "Did they grow up together?"

"I've never asked." He popped another seed in his mouth. "But they're both from Aidenn, so they probably knew each other as kids."

"Wait!" I said, certain I had figured it out. "Are they related?"

Solo laughed. "I hope not. Plus, that would mean you and I would be related . . . and we'd probably already know that."

"Oh, yeah," I said, more confused than ever.

Right then the door to the other room opened.

"Looks like he's feeling better," said Solo's great-grandfather as he shuffled across the room, leaning heavily on his stick.

We moved out of his way and watched as he held a towel under the faucet. He wrung out the extra water with his huge hands and draped it over a drying rack. I glanced toward the door, cracked open just enough for me to see Uncle Ned's arm as he lay in a bed.

"He wants to talk to you," the old man said to me. He pointed at the bedroom. "Go on in and say hello."

Uncle Ned was sitting up in bed, covered by a colorful quilt and leaning against several pillows. He wore old-fashioned long underwear, red with white buttons down the front. The way he slumped made him look extra old, which made me a little sad.

"Hey there, Martin."

"Hey, Uncle Ned. Are you okay?"

"Been better, been worse." He patted the empty space on the bed next to his legs. I sat next to him.

"Are you sick?"

"I have a condition I keep forgetting I've got," he replied and chuckled. "Lots to remember when you get old. Problem is the memory goes first."

He took a slow sip of water from a glass on the nightstand. His hand was trembling, so he had a hard time placing it back on the table.

As I scanned the room, I noticed a large black-and-white sketch tacked to the wooden wall. It showed two men sitting on a rock by the lake. Right away, I could tell the men were Uncle Ned and Isaac.

And all at once I knew why this place felt so

familiar: Uncle Ned's painting of the cabin and goats on the side of a hill grazing under sparkling light. It was the one he'd removed from the easel the day I painted a picture of the rain.

"You gave us all quite a scare, you old geezer," said Isaac as he came back into the bedroom with Solo right behind him.

Uncle Ned reached out his hand and the hermit took it. They stayed like that for a while, holding hands in front of me, gazing at each other. Next thing I knew Isaac leaned on his walking stick, bent over Uncle Ned, and kissed his forehead. I checked to see Solo's reaction. But he just rolled his eyes and smirked, as if it happened all the time.

It was something I had seen my parents do, my dad leaning over my mom and kissing her face, and it was the kind of thing that made me roll my eyes and smirk too.

That's when everything fell into place.

I turned my gaze back to Uncle Ned, who smiled at me, as if answering the question I couldn't ask.

"Do you brave boys mind escorting me down the mountain?" he asked.

"Are you sure you're . . . okay now?" I must've sounded pretty doubtful, because Ned chuckled and said, "Trust me, Martin—if I wasn't, Isaac wouldn't let me out of his sight."

Solo and I waited outside while Uncle Ned "pulled a few loose ends together." We were both extra tired now that our stomachs were full, so we lay down in a grassy area between the sculptures above and the goats below.

As usual, I had about a hundred questions I wanted to ask as we rested side by side, watching the clouds drift overhead.

"How long have they been together?"

Solo's eyes were closed, but I could tell he was awake. "Ever since I can remember."

My next question was the most confusing part for me. It was also the most awkward to ask. "So if Isaac is your great-grandfather, that means he used to be married to your great-grandmother?"

Solo stretched his arm out, plucked a long piece of grass, and stuck it in his mouth.

"What's your point, Martian?" he asked, the long green stalk moving up and down as he chewed the end.

"Well, um," I stammered, trying to find the

words, "did they get divorced?"

He readjusted his arms under his head and looked directly at me. "Everything went bad for Isaac a long time ago. He was living up here with my great-grandma and a bunch of their kids when the police arrested him for something to do with being against the government."

"You mean that part is true?"

Solo turned back and stared up at the clouds. In the distance we could hear tiny goat bells ringing from down below.

"No, he hadn't done anything really wrong, except not pay his taxes for a couple of years. But he got out of serving in Vietnam because of his deaf ear, and that's about the same time he started sending those flashlight signals across the lake. So people got suspicious. They thought he was doing something illegal, sending spy codes or something. He got arrested and by the time he cleared his name, my great-grandma had packed up all the kids and left."

I let everything stew in my brain awhile before I asked, "How come she left him if he didn't turn out to be a criminal?"

Solo rested his arms across his stomach and closed

his eyes. "Geez, Martian. Because she figured out that the signals were actually for Ned."

"*Oh.*"

"And Isaac still feels like people have it out for him. That's why he never leaves the mountain. And why Ned is always up here."

"That's really sad," I said.

Solo shrugged. "I guess. In some ways."

I thought about it a little more and realized I knew what he meant. It *was* a sad story, but some good had come out of it too. There were all the beautiful sculptures Isaac had created. And he and Ned were still together, all these years later.

Once Uncle Ned was ready to go, the three of us headed down the mountain. We moved very slowly and made lots of stops. Solo and I walked on either side of Uncle Ned in case he felt weak and needed our support. By the time we finally reached the edge of the lake, the sun was low in the sky.

"You paddle the canoe over to the tree house, Martian," said Solo. "I'll row Ned in his boat over to the dock."

So that's who owned the old metal rowboat tied to the tree.

Together, we moved silently across the lake, thoroughly exhausted. The air smelled sweet and felt soft. *This,* I thought to myself, *is where I want to be. Forever.*

When we reached Beyond, I waved to Solo and Uncle Ned before I drifted left toward the tree house. Ned saluted me—which made me feel like a hero—as Solo angled the oars and rowed off in the opposite direction.

I waited by the shore long enough to climb up and down the tree house several times, wondering why Solo hadn't returned. After a while I decided to look for him, stopping off first at Uncle Ned's cabin. But the house was quiet and dark. Maybe he had already gone to sleep after such a tiring day. So I continued on along the shoreline, over to the dock. I saw that Uncle Ned's metal row boat was now tied up next to the wooden red *To Beyond and Back* boat—the one used for trips between the island and the mainland. That must mean Aunt Lenore and Tess were back. Tess would be wondering where I'd been . . .

As soon as I entered the kitchen I heard loud

voices in another part of the house, as if people were arguing. I rushed through the dining room and the den, then down the front hall until I burst into the living room.

"*Dad?*"

My father stood in the center of the faded tapestry rug, grimacing, his arms tightly crossed. Uncle Ned and Solo were standing against the far wall, while Tess perched anxiously on the edge of the couch.

Dad's eyes widened, almost as if he was surprised to see me there. Or at least he was surprised by something he saw. "Martin?"

"Why are you here?" I blurted. "It's not the end of July yet. I still have five more days."

Instantly, he frowned again. "I tried calling, but the phone was out!"

"I'm very sorry about that," said Tess, "but the service isn't always reliable up here."

"It's different from living in the city, Jonny," added Uncle Ned.

"I'm well aware of that, thank you," Dad snapped. "We got an invitation to the Jersey Shore this weekend, Martin, so I came a little early. And obviously it's a good thing I did!"

"Mr. Hart," said Tess. "Please, let's calm down and sort this out. Why don't I make us some tea?"

"I'm sorry, Tess, but it's too late for that," said Dad. "Go upstairs and pack your bags, Martin. We're leaving. Now."

CHAPTER THIRTY-THREE

"Why? What's wrong?" I cried. "You were the one who wanted me to come to the island in the first place!"

"But I never expected you to spend your time like *this*," Dad said, pointing at Uncle Ned and Solo. "I know what you've been up to, hanging around that hermit up on the mountain."

"What are you talking about? I just met him today! I went up this morning to help—"

"You've got it all wrong, Jonny," Uncle Ned said quietly. "Martin's telling you the truth. These two boys saved my life."

"What I don't understand, Mr. Hart," said Tess, "is how you knew where they were in the first place. They haven't even had a chance to explain."

"That little girl told me," said Dad, re-crossing his arms.

"What little girl?" asked Tess. "There's no little girl here."

I followed Solo's gaze toward the doorway just as something moved in the hall. That's when I remembered the noise I'd heard the night before, upstairs in one of the empty guest rooms.

Solo moved toward the doorway.

"Clam?" he called out gently.

A second later she rushed into the room and wrapped her arms around his waist. Solo patted his cousin's back and stroked her yellow hair. Somehow, watching them together didn't make me feel as jealous now. I was kind of glad they had each other and that Clam didn't have to face the adults alone.

"Who in the world is *that?*" said Tess.

"Are you telling me you don't even know that a little girl is staying in your house?" Dad shouted at Tess.

"That's Samuel's cousin from the village," Uncle Ned explained. "She's a good kid."

"I don't believe this," said Dad. "What kind of

house are you running here, Tess? You leave Martin alone for who knows how long with these homeless kids who roam the island, not to mention Ned and his . . . " He bit back whatever he was going to say, then plowed on. "This kind of thing never would've happened when Aunt Lenore was in charge!"

"Now that's enough, Jonny," said Uncle Ned. "Don't blame Tess for any of this."

"Or Solo or Clam," I heard myself saying. "They haven't done anything wrong."

Suddenly, Clam broke away from Solo and rushed over to me. She hugged my waist and pressed her face into my chest. Her tiny body was shaking, so I hugged her back. And all at once, the distrust and resentment I'd been holding on to all these weeks melted away.

"Martin, I told you to go upstairs," snapped Dad. But I couldn't move. I couldn't let go of Clam. It was like I had to make up for all the time I had been so mean to her.

"Martin, I said—"

"Dad." I expected my voice to wobble, but it didn't. It sounded amazingly calm, much calmer than I felt. "Please, you need to listen to us . . . "

At that moment the door slammed back against

the wall. Aunt Lenore entered the room wearing a bright red gown. Her white hair stuck straight up in the air. "No one's going anywhere," she announced.

"Aunt Lenore!" Dad grinned nervously. "I didn't mean to—"

"Sit down, Jonathan," she commanded. "I have a few things to say to you."

"Lenore?" said Tess. "You're supposed to be resting."

"Who can rest with all this nonsense going on?"

At that point Solo took Clam's hand and led her toward the door. "Go on," he said gently. "We'll meet you outside in a few minutes."

She turned and ran out of the room, and that's when I realized how much the loud voices must be upsetting her.

"Please, Aunt Lenore," said Dad, moving toward her, "don't get yourself worked up."

She raised her hand to stop him from coming closer.

"Oh, you've already done a dandy job of working everyone up. You've been doing that since you were six years old! Now, I said *sit*."

Dad slowly lowered himself to the couch.

"And for your information," she added, "I'm still fully in charge and haven't lost my mind yet. I'm simply careful about how I choose to use it."

I couldn't believe it—she was confessing her secret in front of everyone!

"Now just what is that supposed to mean?" demanded Tess.

For a second Aunt Lenore seemed to forget how angry she was at Dad. She smiled like a little kid who'd gotten away with something. "I guess you could call it a test. And don't worry, Tess, you've passed."

"A test?" Tess yelped. "What *kind* of test?"

"I had to find out exactly whom I could trust to have my best interests at heart, as well as the best interests of the island. I'd like to believe that my family and friends would honor my wishes, even if my body and my mind gave out. But I couldn't be certain—so I've been running an experiment these past few months. To see how people would treat a dying, demented Lenore. To see who would stand by me and who would try to take advantage of me." She shot a cold look at Dad. "Can you guess what score I gave you, Jonathan?"

Tess looked as if she was about to fall off the couch, but Uncle Ned started to chuckle.

"You may not have lost your marbles yet, sister, but that doesn't mean you're not crazy."

Dad looked as if his brain was working overtime to catch up with all this. "Aunt Lenore, I hope I haven't given you any reason to think that I—"

"That you *what?* That you're only here because you expect to inherit this island when I die? That you've been trying to manipulate me, and your own son for that matter, simply to get what you think you want?"

For a minute, Dad seemed to be at a loss for words. Part of me felt sorry for him—but part of me also thought, *Aunt Lenore's right.* Dad hadn't been honest with any of us. His plans for me this summer had been more about his needs than mine. And now, just because things weren't turning out the way he'd expected, he wanted me to pack up and leave.

Finally Dad took a deep breath. "With all due respect, Aunt Lenore," he said—and I could tell he was straining to hold back his anger—"I'm afraid all of this has been a big mistake. Martin is a very fragile child with a long spreadsheet of issues . . . "

As soon as he started talking, everything that had happened over the past weeks—everything that made me feel a hundred times better about myself— began slipping away, as if a few words of doubt from Dad could erase it all.

But then I looked at Aunt Lenore. At Uncle Ned, at Tess. At Solo. All these people had believed in me this summer. They hadn't made me feel as if something was wrong with me. They'd trusted me. And I'd been fine. More than fine.

"Dad," I said. "It wasn't a mistake. You were right—sending me to Beyond was the best thing you could've done. And now I feel like I belong here. I want to stay."

Once again, my father stared at me as if he didn't recognize me.

"You hear that, Jonathan Hart?" said Aunt Lenore, pointing her long bony finger at my father's nose. "I'm telling you, this young man of yours is one of the most capable, brightest, most interesting boys I've ever known. He has *it!* Joie de vivre! Genuineness! That *golden glow.* Just like young Samuel here."

Solo and I glanced at each other in amazement. No one had ever stood up for us, not like this.

"And, as I told you fifteen years ago, if you can't see beyond your bottled-up, bubble-wrapped life and recognize good, decent individuals the way they are," she continued as she swept her arm toward everyone in the room, "then I suggest you buy a one-way ticket to yesterday and never come back!"

"But—" began Dad as he shrank back into his seat.

"No *buts!*" croaked Aunt Lenore. "Furthermore, Martin will be staying here through August. You can come back for him the weekend before his school year starts. The doctor informed me today that my mind is sound, but my core is fading fast. My days are numbered."

"Oh, don't be so dramatic," murmured Uncle Ned, who still looked amused. "Everyone's days are numbered."

"True enough," said Aunt Lenore, "but mine happen to be counting down a tad faster. So I'd like Martin here at the Great and Beautiful Beyond as long as possible. He needs to learn everything there is to know before he inherits this island."

I'd like to think my dad changed his mind and agreed to let me stay because Aunt Lenore convinced him it was the right thing to do. But maybe he just wanted to make sure I stayed in Aunt Lenore's will. After all, if he couldn't have Beyond, he probably figured that having me inherit it was the next best thing.

Either way, since he had made a reservation at the wet cat motel in Connecticut and hadn't expected to be leaving so late, Dad seemed in a hurry to get going. He promised to call before he returned at the end of August, assuming the phone was working again. Then he rushed out of the house without saying much of a good-bye to anyone.

I followed him out onto the porch, feeling kind of sorry for him.

"Why don't you stay too, Dad? At least for a few days?"

For a second I thought he might, as he glanced up at the broken sign and smiled, but then he checked his watch and shook his head.

"Wish I could, buddy, but I can't."

He gave me an awkward pat on the shoulder, almost as if he wanted to hug me. "See you in a few more weeks, Martin."

I watched as he hurried down the trail and into the woods, heading toward the water.

The funny thing is, before tonight, I would've been excited to show him all the stuff I had learned to do—how well I could shoot a slingshot and climb a rope and paddle a canoe. But now it didn't seem to matter anymore. I didn't feel like I needed to prove anything to him. Maybe the only person I needed to prove anything to had been me all along.

That evening, after the six of us feasted on leftovers in the dining room, Solo, Clam, and I collapsed on the dock together. Mr. Little had joined us too. I introduced him to Clam and asked her if she would like to take care of him. A moment later he was resting snugly in Clam's small hand. I had the feeling he belonged there now.

The gentle sounds of the twilight forest and the rippling waves on the lake soothed our tired bodies, as if the earth were rocking us to sleep.

A rustling sound a few feet away woke me. On the shore, a black figure flapped its wings. I sat up and saw that it was Poe. I hadn't seen him since last night, outside the tree house, which felt like a lifetime ago. I wondered what he was trying to tell me now as he bounced along the lake.

Solo, Clam, and Mr. Little continued to doze as I stepped carefully over them. Poe shook his beak in the air, then sprang in and out of the water. So I removed my shirt and sneakers and entered the dark lake, first to my waist, then my chest, and finally my shoulders. I felt lighter than usual, as if the water were lifting me. A million faded stars shined overhead as I tilted my head back and spread my arms. I released my breath and my legs drifted to the surface. At last, I could float.

Excerpt from "The Raven"
by Edgar Allan Poe

Once upon a midnight dreary, while I pondered, weak and weary,
Over many a quaint and curious volume of forgotten lore—
   While I nodded, nearly napping, suddenly there came a tapping,
As of some one gently rapping, rapping at my chamber door.
"'Tis some visitor," I muttered, "tapping at my chamber door—
        Only this and nothing more."

. . .

Deep into that darkness peering, long I stood there wondering, fearing,
Doubting, dreaming dreams no mortal ever dared to dream before;
   But the silence was unbroken, and the stillness gave no token,
   And the only word there spoken was the whispered word, "Lenore?"
This I whispered, and an echo murmured back the word, "Lenore!"—
        Merely this and nothing more . . .

. . .

Open here I flung the shutter, when, with many a flirt and flutter,
In there stepped a stately Raven of the saintly days of yore;
   Not the least obeisance made he; not a minute stopped or stayed he;
   But, with mien of lord or lady, perched above my chamber door—
Perched upon a bust of Pallas just above my chamber door—
        Perched, and sat, and nothing more.

. . .

But the Raven, sitting lonely on the placid bust, spoke only
That one word, as if his soul in that one word he did outpour.
   Nothing farther then he uttered—not a feather then he fluttered—
   Till I scarcely more than muttered "Other friends have flown
    before—
On the morrow he will leave me, as my Hopes have flown before."
        Then the bird said "Nevermore."

INTERNATIONAL MORSE CODE

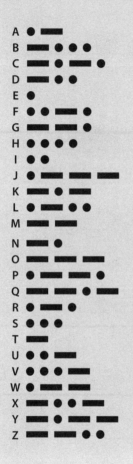

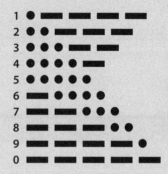

ACKNOWLEDGMENTS

Many people helped tell this story. I'd like to thank my college friend, Joe Tripp, for generously sharing his boyhood experiences with me, as well as my lifelong pals, David Reusch and John Drummey, and my son, Nate Eames. A deep and heartfelt thanks, as always, to my agent, Susan Cohen, and most of all, thank you to my gifted (and very funny) editor, Amy Fitzgerald.

ABOUT THE AUTHOR

Elizabeth Atkinson has been an editor, a children's librarian, an English teacher, and a newspaper columnist as well as a fiction writer. Her novels include the award-winning *I, Emma Freke*. She splits her time between the North Shore of Massachusetts and the western mountains of Maine. Visit her on the web at www.elizabethatkinson.com.